Acclaim for *Baker's*

"Fantastic story. Imaginative, well-researched, nicely detailed, intelligently written. Popular setting and subject matter. Particularly like Professor Melissa White – I want to take her class. It takes confidence to write scenes from the distant past - the 1777 scenes are told quite well. *Baker's Corner* has a lot going for it."

- Michael Biehl
   Author, *Karen Hayes Mysteries*

"Crisp reading indeed, compelling, enthralling, fantastic! I don't think I'll ever taste, or even think, of chocolate again without having a fond thought of *Baker's Corner*."

-Erik Roth
   Editor, *A Nickel & A Nail Productions*

"Loved the way occurrences from the past are woven into the later sections of the story taking place in the modern periods. Would love to have learned more about the tantalizing subplots (i.e. Chris Sebastiene and Ketia's developing relationship) and the intriguing underworld trade. I thoroughly enjoyed the read."

- Jean-Pierre Jacquet
   Educator/Dean (raised in present day "Baker's Corner")

Dedicated to
David Matthew Smith
1951-2011

David
Not the first
Not the last
For there remain
Goliaths on the path

But you stepped forward
Without stone or sling
And with courage love and hope

You sing
For all to hear

© 2015 by J. R. Quirk

The past is never dead. It's not even past.

--William Faulkner

YESTERDAY

CHAPTER 1

**1776
Baie du Port au Prince
West Indies**

With the British concentrating on New York, Hannan was successful in consigning a merchant ship out of New Bedford. The *Vast Trader* bobbed patiently in Baie du Port au Prince while he bargained ashore. The Merchant Marais had the best products West Indies could offer, cacao beans and slaves. Before signing the contract for his cargo, Hannan allowed his lust to interfere.

"There is the matter of the girl. The older of the sisters. You know of whom I speak?"

"Of course," said the trader. Be warned she is very difficult, and will be costly to you. Thrice the usual tariff."

"Adjust the contract. Bring her to my quarters. We sail in the morning."

The Merchant Marais nodded his agreement. Hannan left the shop and walked down the cobbled street as the tropical sun was setting. Against his better judgment he decided to step into a pub for a quick pint even though he knew such a place likely harbored lawless and dangerous men.

The ale was barely to his lips when his judgement prevailed.

"Fine ship that *Vast Trader* mister. Now you don't know me for sure but I have had my eye on you and that ship and I might wonder if you'd do me the courtesy of escorting me on board for a tour tonight? Mister…?"

"Hannan. John Hannan from Boston, sir. And may I inquire as to your business that interests you in my ship?"

"Well, I appreciate fine ships tis all, and fine cargo as well. You might call me a privateer."

"Might?"

"There is the problem of me Letters of Marque having expired, so to say."

"You're telling me you're a pirate then?"

"As I said, you don't know me but I think you know of me. Audette is the name. You see my business is ships. If I like one I acquire it. I control shipping in these parts. Your ship is in my water."

Hannan had heard talk of Audette on the waterfront. The golden days of the buccaneers had long since past, but Audette could easily have thrived in those years such was his fast-made reputation during the first months of the revolution. He had caused the Brits considerable grief as a privateer for the Americans before fleeing to the waters of the West Indies. Hannan was about to resign himself to whatever fate awaited when the businessman in him tried a gambit.

"You say you appreciate fine cargo. Would cacao bean be considered fine?"

"I'd have no use for such. It is cacao bean you've taken as cargo? For what purpose?"

"My associate, the Doctor James Baker, and I have very successful chocolate enterprises in Boston. We are on the verge of making our products world-renowned. I would need to make increasingly frequent trips to this port for purchase of bean. Perhaps Mister Audette would be interested in acquiring a percentage in this venture?"

"How frequent will be your trade then?"

"With one ship perhaps twice a year. Obviously, we'll be needing more ships as we increase production. Would you be willing to invest a ship for say twenty per cent of annual profits?"

"No. But I would be willing to let you sail away and return as often as you like for fifty percent of your purchase funds each visit."

Hannan could not conceal his dismay. "Why that's, that's..."

"Piracy? No that only occurs at sea. This is merely business. Go see the merchant and borrow back half your money. I'll be set right here. Have it to me within the hour and you'll be sailing in the morning. Otherwise we'll be taking that tour of our new ship together."

Audette affixed Hannan such a fierce stare that he could but only hurry wordlessly out the door. Stepping quickly toward the merchant's shop he realized he'd ought to forego his purchase of the girl if he had any hope of meeting Audette's financial demand. But his lustful desire exceeded his business acumen. Back in Boston the price of chocolate was about to increase considerably.

*

She cuddled her two daughters in the dark storage room of the merchant shop where they were permitted to make their bed. Baina, her older daughter was fifteen, Kiskeya thirteen. Marais had come for Baina but Imena resisted. The merchant yielded to the mother but only temporarily. He would be back shortly. He told her he had sold Baina and she must go.

Imena wondered if the terribleness would never cease? They survived the slaughter at their village, the forced march, the ship's belly. They took some small comfort that the merchant acquired them and kept them together to labor in his shop. At first she serviced only Marais and he left the girls alone. But he tired of her and began directing his interest toward Baina, leaving Imena to service his clients. Now his attention is solely with Kiskeya. Baina goes with clients, one of which has apparently purchased her.

They have cried their tears. She tells her daughters to listen as there is little time. She gives a small wood box to Baina. The inscriptions carved on the sides are powerful magic she tells her. The daughters know that their mother was a respected priestess in their village. She may have lost her title but not her craft. And she has been teaching them her magic.

"I have seen this man who comes for you," she says. "We will dream him. I will disfigure his dream shape and make him weak. We will see him that way in our dreams. His evil spirit may travel both worlds and bring him trouble. You will need powerful magic to survive, Baina. Kiskeya and I will find you and help you in the dreams. You must use this box when the time comes. This is how. Listen."

CHAPTER 2

**1965
Codman Square
Dorchester**

The scent of cocoa beans roasting at Baker's Lower Mills factory lifted Finn Leahy's spirit slightly. Arms resting on the Formica kitchen table, he sat in sullen contemplation. He arrived home mid-afternoon to his mother's unkempt third-floor flat in this Southern Avenue three decker and found her passed out drunk on the living room couch with his chain-smoking stepdad mulling about in a foul mood.

Finn was released at noon from his second incarceration in reform school, and was home but thirty minutes when something he said, or didn't say, caused fists to form and a welt to appear under his left eye. Then his stepdad stomped out "to see a man about a horse" at the tavern on Norfolk Street.

From his position near the open kitchen window Finn could see down into the grimy alley and across to the next-door kitchen window fifteen feet away. There his friend Mike lived, or at least was living, when Finn was "sent up" for six weeks to Dorchester Juvenile Hall for taking a neighbor's car on a joy ride and crashing it into a parked Pontiac belonging to another neighbor on Colonial Avenue. Finn didn't think his actions offensive or his neighbors victims. In fact, he didn't think of Southern Avenue and the intersecting streets on the subtle slopes called Codman Square as a neighborhood at all. He thought of it as "juvie hall" without bars. Here he had more freedom to move about, but there was nothing much to do in either space. He always felt trapped. And restless.

Finn was hoping for something he couldn't name. A feeling. Something lost. A sudden summer evening breeze dispersed the delicate cocoa bean aroma and left the kitchen filled with the heavy air of stale smoke and boredom. Finn stood. Slowly he headed out the front door and down the steps into the dubious promise of the evening streets. He was almost fifteen years old, and to him that seemed about as old as anybody could ever get.

*

At the Norfolk Tavern Finn's stepfather, Dennis Dunn, had just finished making a bet in the back room and was heading to the bar when Fat Eddie Mahoney, the local loan shark, entered the tavern. Dunn tried to slip to the shadows and out the door but Mahoney quickly cut him off and bulled him to a dark corner.

"I'll have the money tomorrow Eddie."

"Too late, Dunn. But you got lucky. The boss wants you to take care of a little something for him, and the interest will be forgiven."

"Sure Eddie, you just name it and it's done."

"The something is named Connolly, you know, the ex-cop lives over on Darlington Street. Boss wants you to put a hurt on him. You don't need to know why, just make sure he gets the message that someone is unhappy."

"Ok, thanks Eddie I'm all over it."

"Don't thank me you shithead. Up to me I'd get you a ride down to the marsh. Have you thumped. The boss needs this done real quick and you just happen to be close by. Like I said, you got lucky. Now get outta here, before I find someone luckier."

CHAPTER 3

**1777
The Upper Road
Dorchester**

Looking ahead as he walked along the Upper Road, Hannan eyed James Baker entering the Liberty Tree Tavern as dusk settled upon Dorchester. Pleased that his potential financier arrived at the appointed hour, Hannan quickened his pace and promptly entered the lamp lit interior where he found Baker patiently seated at a corner table. Upon ordering two pints from the barkeep, Hannan removed his cornered hat and greeted the now standing Baker with a firm handshake and his best posture of confidence.

"Well now then am I to suppose another investment proposal is about to unfold on this table?" said Baker as the two men sat down.

"Certainly not before we quaff some ale," said Hannan as he signaled the barkeep to hurry on.

"How is the missus, John, and yourself?"

"She's the same witch as ever, as well you know. As for me, I hope to be much improved when we part this establishment."

Two pints were set hastily on the table causing Hannan to scowl at the back of the departing barkeep who left a considerable amount of his ale puddled on the straw-covered floor.

Hannan swallowed a long pull from his mug and was just beginning his pitch when the proprietor Lemuel Robinson himself entered the tavern to the great attention of all. It was but a year ago Colonel Robinson had successfully led his contingent of patriots, many of whom were presently in the tavern, along with the main body of General Washington's troops to victory over the redcoats at Dorchester Heights. Robinson nodded hello to Baker before joining a crowd at the bar. He ignored Hannan whom he despised for his lack of participation in the effort that caused the British to evacuate, liberating Boston.

Unphased by the slight, Hannan continued his pitch. "Straight to the point James, so as not to waste your time. If you can front the tariff as before, there is window of opportunity, and the means, for me to set sail to the Indies within the next few months. The promise I make is not only will we sustain our chocolate enterprise but double production within a year of my return."

"Ah but John, the high seas present a considerable risk to an investor. With all the hostilities, to say nothing of the chances of simply being lost at sea by act of God. I just don't know, sir, if I can so gamble. It is against my nature and good fortune."

"Yet if I gave you proper assurances that my interests in the business would default to you should such ill fate befall me?"

"Now that would mitigate some, but there is the matter of Mrs. Hannan."

"The bitch shall not present a problem I assure you James." Hannan laughed derogatively. "Fortunately there are some legal mechanisms that avail us so as neither burning nor stoning need be considered alternatives."

"Perhaps then we should call on Mr. Cronin to prepare some papers in the morning, John?"

"Agreed. But I guarantee you any insurance will be rendered useless. For upon my return with a treasure of cacao bean your good fortune to date shall seem paltry."

"I don't doubt you, John. Raise your pint, sir. Here is to your health and your uncanny ability to turn a bean into a delicacy. There are some who would indeed suspect witchcraft at that feat. Drink now and I'll take my leave of you until morning when our business is at hand."

*

Sarah carried the trade goods to Baker's General Store with Mrs. Hannan. She was pleasantly surprised to find herself dismissed from further chores as Mrs. Hannan indicated she had private matters to attend to. There was plenty of afternoon light left so Sarah decided to walk a ways down the south trail away from the store and the Upper Road.

She paused in a field to breathe in the fragrances of spring in full bloom. A particular scent made her think of her birthplace. She missed her mother and sister Kiskeya. She could hear them calling her in the gentle breeze. "Baina, Baina where are you?" Though the Hannans and everyone else called her Sarah, she would never forget her true name, or her family. She would never forget or forgive her abduction by Hannan. She had survived. She had adapted, even learning the language. She would endure.

   She was about to head back when she noticed a figure at the edge of the wood watching her. An Indian emerged into the clearing, raising a hand in acknowledgement. He was much taller than she, and older. Sarah stood frozen in place as he approached.

   "Do not be afraid," he said. "I am here like you. Drinking the salty breeze. Listening to the voices." His tone had a calming effect on Sarah. She visibly relaxed.

   "The ocean is there," he said pointing along the north trail. "Once my people had a village here."

   "My people had a village on the other shore," Sarah said. "It was destroyed. My mother is a priestess. I heard her calling me when you approached."

   "My father's father was Sachem. Chief. Like my father, and most of our people, he died from the sickness brought to our shore. I come here to listen to their songs in the wind and to honor the days when they would walk from the great hills to the fishing grounds." The Indian looked deeply at her and waited until Sarah returned his gaze. "I am Attuck, which means little deer." He laughed because he knew she did not see him as little.

"I am Baina, which means Sarah," Baina Sarah said proudly, and then laughed at herself because she was joking.

"Moswetuset," Attuck said, pointing again to the north trail. "There across the marsh from the place the English now call Pine Neck. It is where we fished in the summer. They have taken it from us. And they have taken our name. Like they surely stole your name."

"They cannot take my name," Sarah said defiantly. "They cannot even speak it."

"We have much in common Baina Sarah," Attuck said. He opened the pouch tied to his waist and removed something. "You say your mother is priestess. Shaman. I too make medicine. Take this. It is strong. Use it as your mother would tell you. Be brave. You have a long journey still."

She looked at the fragment of bone and the piece of crystal in her hand and into his eyes. She realized that despite what she held, it was kindness that he had bestowed upon her.

The Indian nodded, turned and walked into the woods. The ocean and his people behind him.

Sarah walked back past Baker's store and along the Upper Road to the shed where she quartered behind the Hannan home. As dusk settled she sniffed the air one more time before going inside for the night. A breeze from across the great sea found her. She would follow it home in her dream tonight.

*

After James Baker left the Liberty Tree Tavern Hannan finished his ale and made his way to the exit. An unsteady scarecrow of a drunkard with a wayward eye and an evil aura staggered into him despite Hannan's attempt to side step.

"There's ways to take care of witches and bitches mister. But you'll be paying the toll either way, huh?"

Hannan pushed the drunkard aside and hurried outside. *Certainly he could not be speaking directly*, he thought. He had seen this man but once before. It was the night his chocolate mill burned to the ground the previous year just as he had returned from the West Indies. Now Hannan had to rent partnered space from Baker in a Neponset snuff mill to grind and pour his chocolate while Baker's mill thrived down river. The man had vanished before the fire was put out and there was some speculation of arson. At first Hannan suspected Baker had a hand in it, but then decided it was just a careless fire, an act of God. Now uncertainty returned. The reappearance of this man disturbed him greatly, as did his hawkish features. The bastard bore an uncanny resemblance to him. Agitated, he moved quickly through the night along the ridgeline toward his home near the Neponset River. He would take the matter up in the light of the new day.

By the time he got home he had calmed. Noticing the lamplight still burning within the back shed, his thoughts turned to Sarah and he became aroused. He peeked through the cracks in the siding and saw her sleeping. Despite his better judgment, and knowing what wrath his wife might bring, he allowed himself to fall back upon an old habit. He removed his boots and entered the shed.

Sarah did dream of home, but not so sweetly as the breeze that invited her. It was less a dream then a reenactment. In the dream she hid terrified as invading tribesmen killed the village men who resisted, as well as the old who did not. They carried off the screaming children, and then came for the hiding young girls and women. She was quickly found and dragged away by her hair. The man took her to the bush. It happened so fast she could hardly breathe. It was her first time and it hurt deeply in body and soul.

The men tied them together with rope and marched them all night and day, finally crowding them into a dark dungeon where they could hear the sea. The dream allowed her to escape the dungeon with her mother and sister, while the rest of the villagers were boarded on a giant boat that sailed away. She could smell the inviting fragrance in the breeze. It would be all right. But then a man's hand grabbed her from behind and pulled her down. She tried to run but Hannan held her down. Then she awakened. Alone.

After she cried a little, she reached behind her bedding and brought out the small box from her mother. Of course it was no longer hers. She was allowed no possessions. It now belonged to Mrs. Hannan who displayed it proudly on her mantle where Sarah would return it now that she had completed the magic as her mother had instructed.

While Hannan slept off his drink beside her earlier, she went over to his coat and pulled a thread. Near the collar she found a hair. Before closing the box she took some of his fluid from her body and swiped it inside the box with her finger. Then she remembered the bone fragment and piece of crystal. Surely her mother would want her to include them. The spirits of the kind Indian's people would be strong allies. In the morning she would add some ash from the Hannan hearth to the mix and return the box to the mantle. Within a dream she would cast the spell. Hannan and his seed would be cursed.

TODAY

CHAPTER 4

Somewhere in the midden that once resembled the floor of his utility closet, Finn Leahy knew his old Red Sox cap might be found. Reaching blindly he felt a brim just as his hand brushed against something discomforting. Leaving the cap be, he retrieved an odd shaped box. The box.

Fighting back a wave of nausea, Finn pushed it back into the pile and quickly retrieved his ball cap. Finn hated hats. He pulled this one tightly onto his graying skull with his huge laborer hands, as if the cap might block any further thought of the box. He hurried outside.

For Finn's sixtieth birthday Sean got them seats for the night game versus the Yankees. Finn walked the short block from his apartment on Adams Street to the Eire Pub on the corner, where his son was meeting him for a beer before they jumped on the T at Cedar Grove for Fenway.

Finn liked the neighborhood and found it convenient. He'd lived alone in the apartment now for twenty years since his divorce. Marriage wasn't meant for guys like him he figured. But Sean turned out to be a decent person despite all the obstacles he and Ruth had dropped in his path.

"Hey Pops. The hat looks good," said Sean, who also sported a Red Sox cap. "What'll you have?"

"Bud draft Sean. Thanks. Good to see ya."

"Happy birthday you old son of a bitch," Sean toasted with his mug as Finn's promptly arrived.

"Yeah. I'm in prime time now."

Finn surveyed the Eire Pub. One big well lit room with a rectangular bar in the center. He could see several guys he knew by name and several more he knew by their barroom antics. Finn thought of the long defunct Norfolk Tavern that his stepfather frequented and how different a place was the Eire. A "Mens Bar" as it still stated in the engraved woodwork outside, although women crashed the party back in the seventies. Blacks and gays soon followed, but the clientele remained solidly white Irish guys mostly OFD (originally from Dorchester) and the still arriving immigrants with their brogues.

"You know I had a friend named Mike Scanlon when I was a kid. His Dad went senile before he got to my age."

"Like you ain't already started down that road?"

"Alright now. Easy on the old man. I was just thinkin' how when I was about ten he brought Mike and me here for a ginger ale and a roast beef sandwich. Only thing on the food menu at the time I think. Touted to be the best and cheapest in Boston. Maybe still is."

"Think it might be good enough for Obama? Ya know he's coming to town tomorrow. Maybe he might be tempted to drop in and have a bite."

"Because Reagan and Clinton raised a glass here? No, I don't think so. He don't play so well to this crowd. Where's he speakin' again?"

"Codman Square. At the Health Center. Want to go?"

"And what? Take a bullet for him. No thanks."

"C'mon Pops. Times have changed. For the better. Anyways drink up. We gots ta get movin if we wanta see the first pitch."

As they walked to the station Finn thought of how things had changed since his days as a kid in Codman Square and how different was Sean's world. Sean got to go to B.C. High and Harvard. His friends moved in tribes and made lots of money. Finn was simply grateful that he got sent to a trade school where he learned auto mechanics and landed a job so he could steer clear of crime and scrape by. Money? Be lucky if he could put down the wrench and wipe the grease off his hands at seventy. That is if the big banks don't wipe out his paltry 401k plan. Or the Big Mechanic doesn't pull his plug cables.

Growing up in Codman Square Finn had always felt trapped. Never more so then when he finished the court appointed residential school program and returned to his alcoholic mother's flat on Southern Avenue. His stepfather had been sent to prison for a string of minor crimes. Finn was expected to put bread on the table so his mother could spend the little money she had available to supply booze.

The neighborhood had changed fast while he was away and the change accelerated upon his return. He never thought himself a racist but fear of change, fear of other, took its toll on him. In a twisted sort of logic, fight or flight swapped definitions. Typically the fighter, the only way Finn could fight his way out of that situation was by flight. After two months he left Codman Square for good.

He didn't go to the South Shore where the manipulating banks and developers steered the majority of white families. He moved over the hill to the relatively stable Neponset area and found work as a mechanic in a shop on Morrissey Boulevard.

As the years marched by Finn seldom drove through his old neighborhood even though it was less than one mile away. He wouldn't feel safe walking there so he never did. For him Codman Square had ceased to exist. It was lost in time. A space captured by alien third-world invaders. Finn did not acknowledge these impressions as racism, although racists shared his view. The only black friend he ever had was Tony Sebastiene, who he had not seen for over forty years except in his dreams.

Sean and he turned the corner on Milton Street by the cemetery. Finn thought of the night with Tony when he climbed into the tomb. Crazy kid. And the box. He hadn't thought about that in decades. Until today when it surfaced from the rubble of his closet.

"Hey Sean, did I ever tell you about the time as a kid when we robbed a grave?"

Sean shook his head exaggeratively. As if to say, 'Not another story, Pops.'

*

Sergeant Antoine "Tony" Sebastiene positioned himself stage right, front row. He didn't wear his Boston PD uniform although he was technically on duty. He elected to stash his gun belt and put on his more appropriate Codman Square Health Center Security jacket. That allowed him to move right to the front without issue. He did work here part time after all. He probably would work here until he turned seventy, but he did plan on turning in the BPD badge and start pulling down his pension this year.

As expected, President Obama worked the friendly crowd, mostly black, into a frenzy with his well-rehearsed call and response delivery. He mentioned how both Lincoln and Kennedy travelled through Codman Square when visiting Dorchester. He spoke of General Washington and his troops staging here for victory and later celebrating at the Liberty Tree Tavern just a few blocks away. Without referencing the beer-sipping visits by two other presidents, he placed both himself and the neighborhood in loftier company. To Tony's surprise the President finished by leaping down the steps and into the crowd right beside him. As the crowd crushed forward Tony and he exchanged a high five before the lithe man moved along the line and was gone.

It didn't surprise Tony that the President chose Codman Square for his Boston visit. The Health Center stands on one of the nation's first "highways". The Upper Road was built in 1654 at the intersection of a pre-European Indian Trail that extended from the Blue Hills along Norfolk Street and down Centre Street to the salt marsh near Port Norfolk, which was once called Pine Neck. Upper Road was renamed Washington Street in 1789 after the first President's inauguration. Across the street stood the James Baker residence and general store. By 1803 the intersection came to be called Baker's Corner honoring the merchant's prominence and commercial influence, especially in the chocolate industry. The intersection was re-named Codman Square in 1848 commemorating the Puritan reverend who delivered fire and brimstone sermons at the adjacent Second (Congregational) Church for over forty years.

Tony found Codman Square to be a fascinating place. It bothered him that so few others gave it the recognition it deserved. So few took the time to learn the history as he did. Of course he'd had the time. He'd lived here all his life and had no intention of dying anywhere else. There were days when he could stand in certain places and feel as if he was transported to another time. Or maybe it was more like time ceased to exist and he could feel the presence of all the souls who travelled this space. It was as close to spiritual as Tony ever experienced.

YESTERDAY

CHAPTER 5

1965
Codman Square
Dorchester

It was another hot summer day, perhaps the last, as it was Labor Day weekend. School would start on Thursday and everything but the weather signaled change. Tony was outside with his sister, both of them hoping to catch a breeze on the steps to the three decker house the Sebastienes shared with two floors of Puerto Rican families. Tony's skin was lighter than some of the Puerto Rican kids but his features were unmistakably African. While they all had to fight for their territory, Tony found himself on the defensive just because of his features. His friends, mostly Irish kids, liked him and looked out for him well enough. Mostly it was the older Irish brothers who taunted and tormented him. His Mom said it was because they were the first dark-skinned family to move into the neighborhood and word got out that if more came then the property values would go down. The older kids were reflecting their parents fear, she said. The younger ones were more forgiving of change because it was all they knew.

"Let's go to Lena's, buy us popsicles," his younger sister Elise implored.

"Nope. Its too hot to walk that far."

"Look. There goes Jack Connolly," Elise said pointing toward the street corner. "He's cute."

"He's white."

"So. That don't make no difference. Maybe I'll marry him."

"Yes it does. No you won't. You gotta marry a Haitian."

"Only Haitians I know are our cousins. Mom says you can't marry cousins."

"What are you two jabbering about?" Mrs. Sebastiene said, as she came up behind them.

"Elise wants to marry Jack Connolly. Maybe you should remind her that they're only ten years old, even if he wasn't white."

"Elise can marry whoever she wants, when she's old enough. Now who's going to walk to the market with me?" Mrs. Sebastiene said. She got no response. "Be a shame if I had to stop by Brigham's for an ice cream cone all by myself."

Elise took the bait. Mother and daughter left Tony alone at his stoop duty.

There were Jews, Greeks, Italians, Portuguese, Armenians, Puerto Ricans, and Irish, plenty of Irish, in Codman Square but few Negroes. Or Haitians either. Tony's mom said they weren't Negroes because they didn't come from the south where the slaves were freed by Abraham Lincoln. Sure they were colored and descended from Africans, but she was born in Haiti and was more French than anything else, she said. Well there weren't any French on Millet Street either. Tony remembered there were plenty of dark skinned people in

Roxbury, where they lived when he was little, before his father left them when he was five. His mom said they moved to Millet Street to have a better chance and go to better schools. Tony never thought much about black or white until they moved to Dorchester six years ago. He had never heard the nigger word directed at him before then either.

He sat quietly for a minute or two. Then he sauntered off to the schoolyard to join whoever might be up to whatever.

*

Finn's stepfather, Dennis Dunn, left the Norfolk Tavern and walked toward the center corner in Codman Square where the bums passed the day along with a shared bottle. He hoped he could find one sober enough to do the Connolly job for him. He was going to pay one of them to deliver a threat. But he hadn't figured out how to "put a hurt on" Connolly along with the message like Fat Eddie Mahoney had told him. He got only as far as the corner liquor store where he saw two young delinquents out front when it came to him. Get to Connolly through his kid.

"Hey mister, buy us a bottle of Thunderbird?" one of them said.

He'd seen this tall one, sixteen maybe fifteen years old, a couple of times with Hanna, a guy at the tavern who did occasional dirty work for Mahoney. Perfect, he thought.

"Sure will kid. And I'll pay for it and throw in an extra five spot, but you gotta do me a favor first."

"What?" said the surly smaller one.

"I need you to rough someone up a little bit. And give him a message. You do that?"

"Maybe" said the tall skinny one with a sick smile that the little one weakly mimicked. "Pay the toll either way."

"Fucks that supposed to mean? Now listen. Only blue house on Darlington Street. A kid about ten lives there. Jump on him when he comes out into the streets. Hurt him but not too much. Let him know it was because his father is being stupid."

"When? Now?" the tall one said.

"Soon as he gives you the chance. Meet me here this time tomorrow. You tell me its done and you get the money. And the wine."

"Get us some TBird now," the little one demanded.

"Get outta here," Dunn said. "Screw."

*

Frank Connolly purchased the blue house on Darlington Street while he was still on the force and times were better. His marriage with Irene was becoming strained. Their kids, young Jack and older sister Annie, knew nothing but the happiness of youth.

Annie Connolly had just turned fifteen and loved everything about life. This summer boys had finally discovered her. When she walked to Codman Square they appeared out of the alleys and off the stoops like she was a magnet. Most were too shy to do other than follow at a distance. Often they would move in a small group and the bravest would call something out. Mike Scanlon was different. He would come to the house and ask for her. They would sit out front and talk. He would kid her about things she said or did. She would happily laugh along with him because he was so gently focused on her. It seemed like they agreed on just about everything. He was meeting her this afternoon here at Brigham's for a frappe. It would be their first date, although he didn't call it one.

She saw Mike walk past her into Brigham's and quickly scan the tables and counter. He was probably relieved to see that none of the guys were present.

"Hey there you!" she called from a booth behind him in that perfect frequency meant only for him.

Enchanted, he spun around smiling, "Hey Annie, what you hiding on me for?" He slid into the bench across from her. He stared knowing he would cause her Irish face to involuntarily blush. It did as she laughed and pulled on her long red hair.

Annie ordered a chocolate banana split and Mike a coffee frappe. They filled each other in on what they had been up to in the eternity since they had last seen each other yesterday. Then Annie turned serious.

"How's your dad?"

"Not too good."

"It's not fair. My dad is probably the same age and he doesn't seem old. You know he used to be a cop but he says your dad is the one he'd want backing him up in a room full of bad guys. Well at least that was before…"

"That's because Dad was a war hero. He went behind enemy lines alone on special missions and got a medal."

"Maybe they'll find some sort of vaccine, like with polio that will fix him."

"Vaccine never fixed anyone who already had polio. Anyway they better be quick because he's gotten so much worse, so fast. He was already starting to forget stuff last spring when Mom died. Then it was like he didn't want to remember anymore. My Aunt Noreen had to move in with us. And he's only like fifty-five or so. I mean aren't you supposed to be really old to be going senile? Like eighty or something?"

Mike paid the check when they left. Annie half-heartedly tried to pay her share. She knew that yielding to Mike made it a real date. He offered to buy her a bag of popcorn from the horse drawn cart on the corner but she was too stuffed to accept. They looked in store windows at new styles and at Thom McCann shoes. They laughed at the jackets in Jordy's clothing store. Mike admitted that he and Tony got their mothers to buy them ridiculous velour jackets with velvet collars there a couple of years ago.

"Promise me you'll never wear that in public with me ok?" she teased.

She jokingly offered to buy him a pencil from the one-legged veteran selling them from his usual spot on a blanket in front of Woolworths.

They laughed as they past him. Only adults continued to be fooled. Finn and Mike staked him out from the roof months ago. They told everyone they knew about how they saw him get up and limp away in the evening shadows when the Square was clear of people, dragging his crutches across Washington Street. He wasn't limping because he was missing a limb but because the one he sat on all day was numb.

As they walked down the hill on Southern Avenue to Annie's house on Darlington Street, they held hands for the first time. For Mike it was an act of bravery because others would undoubtedly notice and only torment could follow. For Annie it was similar but mostly just overwhelming. It was the first sensual experience either had ever had with the opposite sex. They both suddenly discovered that unforgettable threshold of love and sexual attraction for which they had no such description. Either of them would tell you that it was the other who took up their hand, but they could never speak of that, and would never be sure.

*

"There you are. Joe, you're not supposed to wander off like this. What am I gonna do with you?"

Joe Scanlon turned his undivided attention away from the one-legged pencil vendor to where the voice was coming from behind him. A woman. Familiar.

Wife? No. Sister. Yes.

"Joe? C'mon let's walk home," said his sister Noreen as she tussled his wavy gray hair and steered him in the direction of Southern Avenue.

"I know this guy," said Joe refusing to move further and staring intently back down at the vendor who chose to pay no attention to the current activity above him.

"Sure you do Joe. Pencil guy has been there for years. Now let's move on, we're blocking the sidewalk."

She finally got him moving and steered him through Codman Square. But until she got him out of the people flow, and turned back down the Southern Avenue hill toward their flat, there would be more faces to recognize. In the last few weeks Joe began seeing almost every face as familiar. Everybody on television was an old friend, or someone he used to live with. He could never quite pinpoint who the friend was, or where they had lived, but he was sure. It would be amusing if you were anybody but his main care provider. Exactly what Noreen Scanlon realized she was becoming for her brother.

The imagined friends, or the wanderings up to the Square, didn't bother her so much as the hallucinations Joe recently began having two or three times a week. He would get agitated and argue with someone who wasn't there. She could usually talk him back to reality. Her nephew, Joe's son Mike, was better at it. Noreen found the episodes frightening.

Noreen checked the traffic as they were about to cross Talbot Avenue. Over by Kaspar's Market she noticed two men in an animated conversation. One was their shiftless neighbor, Dennis Dunn. The other, a lanky ugly man, she had never seen before.

"There's that fuckin' bastard," said Joe. And he began to get agitated.

"That's Mr. Dunn, our neighbor."

"No the other guy. That fuckin' bastard."

Noreen calmed him down. They crossed the street and made their way home.

Mike was still smiling about the kiss Annie sneaked onto his cheek as they said their goodbyes at her doorstep. In a fleeting image he saw an older Annie holding his hand from bed as she lay there dying. He brushed the inexplicable thought away and continued walking home. Up ahead he noticed Annie's little brother Jack about a block up Southern Avenue. Jack Connolly was ten. Mike knew him as a good kid who'd probably become one of the few success stories of this troubled neighborhood.

Turning on his pocket transistor radio he quickly lost himself in a Red Sox game as Dick Radatz climbed upon the mound to try to close a rare win over the perennial champion Yankees. As he was about to turn the corner he saw something not quite right that drew him away from the game. Up the street little Jack was in some sort of confrontation with a tall skinny boy about fifteen, and another kid Jack's age but shorter. The tall one was holding Jack still while the short one was reaching up and burning Jack's earlobes with a lighted cigarette. Before even hearing Jack's call for help, Mike began jogging toward the trio yelling, "Hey, what are you doing. Stop!" As he closed distance the two assaulters released Jack and ran off.

Mike walked little Jack the short distance to his home. Jack touched his ears and tried not to cry.

"Ever see those bullies before?" Mike said.

"Nope" said Jack, "and I hope I never do again. Thanks for helping me."

"No problem. If they show up around here again let me know and we'll kick their ass. I'll take the skinny guy. You can take the midget, Jack. Deal?"

"Deal" said Jack, tears beginning to stream as he dashed up the stairs to his front door.

"Hey Jack!"

"Yeah?" replied Jack, ashamed to look back.

"Tell your sister I said she's the prettiest girl in Codman Square."

CHAPTER 6

**1777-1807
The Upper Road
Dorchester**

By summer's end it was apparent to all that Sarah was with child. Suspecting that it was her husband who impregnated the girl, Elizabeth Hannan grew increasingly hostile to her. Already a vitriolic marriage, quarrels around the Hannan household became just short of murderous. John Hannan vehemently denied the child was his and implied that it likely belonged to his apprentice Nathaniel, who had taken an interest in the girl. Hannan spent long shifts at his mill followed by drunken hours at the Liberty Tree Tavern. Sarah was no longer of interest to him. In October, having procured the funding from Baker and undertaken final preparations, he set sail again for Baie du Port au Prince from New Bedford.

With Hannan off to sea and Elizabeth mostly avoiding her, Sarah had considerable time of her own, a luxury she had never known. She spent long hours with Nathaniel. She was not certain that the child within her was Hannan's because she had also been with Nathaniel. He was kind and she had grown fond of him. If her child's father is Hannan she hoped it would not be cursed. Perhaps she had cast her spell after the child came to be in her. Perhaps Nathaniel is the father. She had decided that he would be. She told him so. Because he was good.

The child arrived that winter and Sarah called her Adama which meant "Queenly" in her native tongue. Nathaniel named her Katherine, but did not object to Sarah's choice as a nickname. At her request he had in fact taken to calling Sarah by her real name occasionally. "My sweet Baina," he would say in private moments.

There was growing sentiment against keeping slaves in Dorchester. By treating Sarah as a wife Nathaniel freed her in the eyes of the local churchmen. Elizabeth Hannan was relieved and voiced no objection. While the couple was not scorned, they were at best tolerated. It helped that Katherine was light skinned, and growing more beautiful each month.

Word came that John Hannan was lost at sea. Some said he had fallen into a trap set by Audette the privateer. Others spoke of a shipwreck. A few speculated that he had fled back to Ireland to escape his intolerable wife.

When she moved in with Nathaniel, Sarah discretely reclaimed from Hannan's mantle the small box bestowed by her mother. She would take it from her hiding place from time to time and repeat the words her mother had told her. Others could say what they will. She knew that Hannan had fallen to her curse.

Elizabeth Hannan seemed determined to keep her husband's chocolate mill profitable with Nathaniel as her workhorse. Try as he might he could not stop her from ruining the business with her misguided and wasteful directives. He walked out on her after a few months and went to work for Baker.

James Baker moved quickly. With legal documents and cash he was able to buy out Elizabeth and consolidate the chocolate mills. He promoted Nathaniel immediately. Profits soared.

Nathaniel and Sarah grew modestly wealthy. They built a home on the Upper Road not far from the Liberty Tree Tavern. Katherine married a handsome young craftsman named William Preston. The young couple moved into a modest home also on the Upper Road where Katherine gave birth to a beautiful girl.

Before Nathaniel died he gave his daughter Katherine a certificate of interest in some shares he had acquired in Baker's mill. Sarah died soon after her husband, but not before passing along a box to Katherine and certain instructions.

Katherine would often tell her young daughter tales of a Queen Adama and her great powers. They would hold the box sometimes. And like her mother and her mother's mother, she taught her daughter how to dream.

CHAPTER 7

**1965
Codman Square
Dorchester**

Finn lumbered up Southern Ave toward the Whittier School to see what might be happening in back at the fire escape where everybody his age hung out on summer nights.

Some of the usual gang were there but Finn hesitated when he saw the skinny boy and his little companion. He was about to duck back around the corner before anybody saw him, but just then Tony yelled "Hey look who's back from the resort! Finny baby how you doin'?"

Finn put on his best wise-ass face and strutted toward the small group. The skinny boy held a brown bag and was busy inhaling model airplane glue vapors. The little kid was zonked and could barely stand. Neither had noticed Finn's arrival.

Finn was relieved to see Tony jogging over to greet him. Everyone liked Tony, which Finn could never figure out because at fourteen he wasn't very big. And he was colored in a neighborhood where might and white were usually right. Finn signaled Tony back to the corner and led him out of the schoolyard. "You know those glueheads, Tony?"

"Nah. They just wandered in earlier this afternoon and started asking questions. Wanted to know how to find Darlington Street. Now they're back offering to share the shit in that bag, and their bottle of TBird. Can you believe it? No takers here, man."

Walking past Papooies house, the old Greek whose real name they could not pronounce and whom they occasionally tormented just out of boredom, Finn said with less bravado then he would have liked, "The skinny guy was at juvie with me. He's crazy. Says he has killed people. Least that's how he brags."

"C'mon, that fucka can't even fight his way out that paper bag. If he was a killer they never would have let him out. You know?"

"Yeah, maybe you're right. Hey let's go to Lena's. Get an RC. You don't get tonic at juvie unless it's your birthday or somethin. They call them sodas."

"Kaspar's is closer," Tony said.

"Lena's is colder," Finn said.

The old Greek, whose real name was Angelo Papoulias, opened his front door slightly and guardedly surveyed the street.

"Papooey" both boys yelled out, startling the old man as they trotted off to Lena's Variety Store.

*

Finn and Tony leafed through the Superman comics at Lena's Variety Store. When she wasn't looking they nervously peaked inside VU Magazine at gloriously naked breasts. Despite being ancient and hobbled, Lena was keenly observant and had them well within her scan when the bell attached to the door rang as Mike Scanlon entered the store.

"Hello there young man," said Lena, who favored him for some reason and often gave him free penny candy when he was younger.

Mike noticed Finn and Tony over by the magazines looking guilty and excited. He guessed one of them used the entry distraction to stuff a titty magazine up his shirt. They all moved to the tonic chest and pulled RC Colas from the icy water.

Lena asked Mike how his father was doing while returning fifteen cents from his quarter. Mike mumbled "Not great but thanks," and managed a small smile before heading out the door with his buddies and across Talbot Avenue.

Mike was a full year older than his friends. And taller. That plus a natural confidence made him the leader.

"Finn, glad to see ya home from vacation. Ya gotta choose one place or the other and stay put, man. How about that house next to me. You know, your house? That way me and Tony can hang out with you regularly. Right Tony?"

"Sure. Hanging out is cool," said Tony. "My uncle left some beers in the fridge and I put them down the cella before my mother knew they were there. We should hang out at the graveyard and go drinkin' tomorrow night."

"Way to go, man" said Finn slapping palms with Mike then Tony. "Whad'ya score?"

"Knickabocka."

"No shit. Wait. Hey look! They got a ambulance front a the old lady witch house," Finn pointed out excitedly.

The three of them ran a half block down Talbot Avenue just in time to see an old black woman being carried down the front steps roped to a kitchen chair.

"It is so sad. She just can't take care of herself anymore. Her cousin is having her committed," they overheard one of the gathering onlookers say to another.

Finn was elated. "They're taking the fuckin' witch to the nut house!" he practically yelled.

Finn periodically would lead anyone who would follow into the backyard of her three decker where he would taunt the old woman until she emerged on the second floor back porch uttering profanities and strange curses. He could work her up real good. She started keeping a bowl of fluid out back which she would hurl at her tormenters. One time Tommy Mills got hit. His eyes stung and his clothes stank. That was when they discovered the bowl was always filled with her piss.

Tony watched as Finn went on acting like he just won a stick ball game or something. They didn't share his enthusiasm. It seemed that he felt somehow wronged by the woman. Tony didn't feel right picking on the old woman, especially her being one of the only blacks in the neighborhood. He never participated.

Mike had participated in the taunting at first, but the novelty quickly wore off. Recently he began to see the woman not as a witch, but as mentally disturbed. Now he could see clearly that she had been travelling on the same road as his father, only further along. Still he disliked her. He feared her as much as any horror movie monster.

"Gotta go. Graveyard tomorrow night after I get back from visiting my cousins about seven-thirty. Right?" Tony said as he turned away from them toward home

"We'll swipe some ice from the fish market. Wouldn't want to drink warm beer," Mike said.

"Warm beer ain't so bad," Finn said.

The two of them walked together in silence to their neighboring houses. Mike thinking how Finn could never get enough, yet would always be satisfied with less.

CHAPTER 8

Early in the morning there was a knock and Mike opened the front door surprised to see Annie there.

"Why didn't you tell me about Jack and the bullies?"

Mike never saw Annie cross at him before. He felt defensive standing confrontationally with her on his front steps.

"I figured it was between us guys. Heck Annie, he was embarrassed and fighting tears. What was I supposed to do? Run up the stairs. Ring your bell. Say hey, Jack just got picked on and I saved him?"

"Yes."

"That'd be like telling on him and bragging at the same time."

"You think my Mom was gonna not see the burns on his ears?"

" I didn't think about that."

"You know why they burned his ears?"

"No. You?"

"They had a message for him to give my dad. The burns were the message. I've never seen my dad so mad. You should have told me."

"Annie I …," but she was already stomping off in an Irish fury.

"Who's there?" his father called from the kitchen.

"Its ok Dad. I got it."

Mike was supposed to stay home with him until his aunt returned from her errands. They rarely left him alone anymore. Soon after his wife's death, Joe Scanlon's spinster sister moved in with them. At first it was to take care of Mike, which he resisted. Now it was becoming almost a full time job for both of them looking after Joe.

"How about some coffee, Dad? You like that?"

"Sure. And maybe some bakery round bread and baked beans?"

"Alright. I'll run up to the square and get some. Here start with the coffee."

Mike figured he could catch up to Annie on his way to the bakery. Make it right somehow.

"Be right back. Dad," he said as he grabbed his father's wallet from the bureau. In his haste he neglected to shut the front door behind him when he left.

With his full head of wavy hair, albeit gray, and muscular build, Joe Scanlon looked considerably younger than his fifty-five years of age. He was just starting to grapple with the doctors' diagnosis of early dementia when his wife, Helen, died in May.

Joe focused his attention on the open door. He took a sip of coffee and then moved to his bedroom.

Where I am I going?

He found some cash in his sock drawer and keys in the night table drawer.

Where is my wallet? Did I stock the truck camper?

He picked up a framed picture of his wife Helen taken with him at the beach. He wrapped a towel around it. He walked out the open front door and started down the steps when he became confused. He sat down, opened the towel and became lost in the photo.

*

Annie walked fast at first and then slowed. She'd walked blocks in no particular direction or destination. She felt bad at taking her anger out on Mike. She decided to go back and apologize. She found Joe Scanlon sitting on the front steps with the front door open.

"Mr. Scanlon you okay?"

Who is this girl?

"You left your front door open. I'll shut it for you."

She called inside for Mike. There was no answer so she closed the door making sure it remained unlocked.

A woman carrying a grocery bag had paused on the sidewalk. She was asking Joe something but he wasn't listening.

"Annie is anything wrong?"

"I don't think so Mrs. Steinman. I came by looking for Mike. Mr. Scanlon was just sitting there with the door open and flies were getting in his house and all."

Flies. Not fireflies. Not here. Where?

Suddenly Joe was clear. He smiled at the woman, stood up and patted Annie on the shoulder.

"We're going to the beach," he said.

CHAPTER 9

The afternoon sun filtered through the block windows hazily illuminating the space where Frank Connolly sat on a stool. His view was readily interchangeable within any barroom in Codman Square. Dark. Dank. Depressing to anyone who had not imbibed sufficiently.

Connolly had been a Boston cop before he got put out on disability and took up working night security, part-time at the Fine Arts Museum warehouse. With so much free time on his hands he took to drinking more that he should have. He spent most afternoons at the Norfolk Tavern, while his wife Irene put in hours as a bookkeeper at the Baker Mill.

He also liked betting on the horses and had gotten himself considerably behind with the book. Fat Eddie Mahoney covered him until this thing about leaving the door unlocked at the warehouse came up. Frank blew him off. No way he said. But Mahoney persisted saying Jimmy the Boss wanted it to happen. And now just for emphasis they burned his kid's ears for chrissake.

Looking up from his beer he saw Mahoney slide onto the next stool.

"Come near my kid again and you're dead."

"Threatening me Connolly will do you no good," Fat Eddie said. "Like I told you already, this is bigger than both of us."

"I'll kill you, come near him."

"Set it up tonight Frank. Don't be stupid. You didn't leave the door open last night like I told you. Apparently you didn't get the message. Now you will."

Mahoney stood and stepped out the door, the incoming light blinding an already unfocused Frank Connolly.

*

The woman and the girl herded Joe back into the house and left.

I know that girl. Where from? The beach? That's right I'm going to the beach. See some fireflies near the marsh. Go back again.

Joe headed out and up the narrow drive to the back where the old truck with the big camper shell he built on back was parked. It took him awhile to turn the engine over. He let it idle.

He drove along Washington Street heading toward Lower Mills pretty much on automatic pilot. He was passing the Norfolk Tavern when he recognized the lanky guy going inside.

I'm gonna kill that bastard.

Suddenly enraged, Joe stopped the truck in the middle of the street. Cars behind him immediately started honking. He looked ahead and saw a parking space. With great difficulty he maneuvered the truck into the tight space. He had a headache. He felt exhausted. He couldn't remember where he was going. He sat behind the wheel a long while. He napped. He dreamed he was trying to look at the photo he kept of his dead wife, Helen. But he couldn't because flies kept getting into his eyes as a dark woman watched. He awoke in a sweat wondering where he was, what day, what time. He fell back asleep. He dreamed again. He had all the time in the world.

CHAPTER 10

First thing Frank Connolly noticed when he got to work was the black hearse in the lot. Frank's routine at the museum warehouse was simple: sit, read, look. About once per hour he would walk the perimeter of the storage facility and rattle the door locks. This is what he was doing when a sedan pulled into the lot, lights out. He got a look at the driver. At first he thought it was Fat Eddie Mahoney because that was his expectation. But no, this guy was thin, scarecrow thin. A couple of thugs were out of the car on him before the car even stopped moving. Their faces were mostly concealed with bandanas.

"Now you're gonna open that door," said the thug who held the gun to his head. And better be no alarm. Then finish your shift early. Go home. Check on your family."

"And don't be stupid" said the gunman moving toward the hearse as the sedan drove away.

Frank realized he had been stupid. He'd underplayed Fat Eddie as a low-level loan shark, which he was. Somebody bigger actually was squeezing them both. Why? The museum didn't store valuable art in the warehouse. This was all donated stuff or pieces being de-accessioned for auction. His job was mainly to provide authorized access during evening hours. All-night warehouse security was provided with the alarm system, and the late night vehicle patrols of the permanent guards. Somebody must have got something wrong.

He quit his shift early at nine-thirty. He left the alarm off and door unlocked. What else could he do? He had a bad feeling about this. He was worried sick that even though he did what he was told, his family may still be in jeopardy.

As he drove away from the museum he glanced in the rear view mirror and saw the black hearse back up to the warehouse dock.

*

The guys with the hearse moved quickly through the warehouse with flashlights.

"What is this shit? According to Jimmy, supposed to be a three by six crate right inside the door. Unmistakable, he said. Marked fragile."

"Over here," said the other from the rear of the warehouse.

They shined their lights as he pulled away a tarp.

"That's only three by three," said the guy in charge.

"Marked fragile," said the other.

"Load it up," said the guy in charge.

*

Someone had added four feet of chicken wire above the eight-foot high chain link fence separating the schoolyard from Codman Burial Grounds. It was a futile effort to discourage the latest generation of teenage drinkers from desecrating the hallowed grounds.

Codman's tomb was the most prominent, a grass-covered knoll with an iron vault door under the shade of a magnificent oak. Periodically someone would tie a rope from an upper branch so the revelers could swing from above the vault between swigs of beer. The groundskeeper would cut the rope down, pick up the empty bottles and the cycle would begin again.

Tony, as promised had delivered the Knickerbocker beer. It had been chilling all evening in a cardboard carton filled with the ice donated by the unknowing fish market.

"That's the last bottle. Gotta get home before midnight or my mother will be up smelling my breath," said Tony.

"My old lady passed out hours ago," said Finn. "How about you Mike? Your Aunt wait up for you?"

"Naw. She's got my Dad to worry about. He went somewhere in the old camper truck while I was supposed to be watching him. I really screwed up. I suppose she has the cops looking for him by now if he hasn't come back."

"Cops are always looking for my stepdad," Finn said with a chuckle that disguised the emptiness of his home life. He wished he had a strong, caring mother like Tony. Or a real father. Like Mike had, even if the old man was going bonkers.

"Nobody has a truck with a camper except your Dad. Man that was great the time he took us to the beach overnight," Tony said.

"I think he invented the part with the bed over the roof and the escape hatch on top," Mike said.

"Look over there! Here comes someone," Tony said. He pointed toward the cemetery gate.

At the entrance over on Norfolk Street they could see a vehicle entering the graveyard with lights out. The driver paused as a shadowy figure got out and shut the gate behind the vehicle.

"Not just a car," observed Mike. "Looks like a hearse. Must be getting something set up for the morning. Here it comes. Get down."

They lay down on the knoll as the hearse drove toward them and stopped right at Codman's vault.

Tony started to hyperventilate.

"Shh," Finn whispered.

Two men got out. They lifted a crate from the vehicle and put it down. One walked straight toward the tomb. Proned out on the knoll the boys were barely concealed. The man disappeared below from their view. They heard the sliding of metal and the creaking of the old iron vault door opening.

Then the man rejoined the other who held a small flashlight while they rifled through the contents of the crate.

"What's all this shit?" the guy with the flashlight said.

"Sure as hell ain't dope," the other said.

"What we gonna do?" said the guy with the flashlight.

"What we was told to do. Put the crate in there and shut the door."

The two men lifted the crate.

"Somebody's got some explaining to do before the pick up tomorrow or we'll be screwed," the one in charge said as he closed the vault door. "Let's go."

The engine started. The boys lay frozen until they were sure the hearse had cleared the gate.

"I'm gonna have a look at that crate," Finn said.

"You crazy? C'mon guys let's get out of here," Tony said.

But Finn was already moving toward the crypt undeterred. Mike was inclined to follow so Tony joined them at a distance. Mike also held back as Finn slid the bar and pulled open the creaky door. Opening a tomb at midnight was more than a bit creepy. A musty smell rushed out. Mike felt nauseous and retreated a few steps. He and Tony had never gotten into any of the cars Finn borrowed for joy rides. Going in the tomb was even more forbidding. Finn's thrills were often too risky for the others. Tony was already headed for the fence as Finn went in.

"It is totally dark in here. I can feel the crate but it is too heavy to move. Come help me guys."

No response.

"OK then. I'm gonna open it."

"Careful where you put your hands man," Mike warned.

Finn hesitated. What was he doing alone at night in a dark tomb? Fear gripped him and he wanted to run away, fast. Fight or flight. Familiar ground. But Finn did what Finn always did. He stayed. He ran his hand along the dimension of something he could not see. Three by three. About right. He opened the crate. He could feel objects of many shapes and sizes. He settled on a small rectangular item and freed it from the rest. Now he could run. And run he did. The others were already climbing back over the fence.

CHAPTER 11

A Cadillac pulled alongside the hearse in the empty parking lot of the closed Zayre's store.

"Someone is screwing with us," said the driver of the hearse to the shadowy figure who had just lowered the passenger window of the caddy.

"We got the only crate in the warehouse. Smaller than it was supposed to be. We opened it before we stashed it. No dope in there, just museum junk."

"Jimmy's not gonna like this," the shadowy voice said. "Let's go see Fat Eddie," he told his driver.

*

"Where's Fat Eddie?" Frank Connolly said.

"Left with two guys in a caddy about twenty minutes ago. He'll be back. He does a good business right before closing time," said the bartender at the Norfolk Tavern.

"What'll ya have?"

"Shot of CC and a Gansett."

Frank tossed the whiskey and settled in with the beer and his thoughts awaiting Mahoney's return. He'd expected to find Annie safe at home when he got there but she wasn't. He said nothing to his wife who was just beginning to show the routine concern about a teenager staying out so late without calling. Something was wrong.

Fat Eddie Mahoney entered the bar, took a table in the corner and signaled Frank to come over.

"I figured you might come here looking for your daughter," said Mahoney. "She ain't here, and I don't know where she is."

"What do you know? Mahoney?"

"I know you were stupid to get her into this. I know some guys arranged a dope drop through someone inside the museum. I know they didn't get it as planned."

"I left the place wide open for them, like they said."

"But the stuff got switched out or something. They think you set them up."

"Listen I don't know anything about any of this. Is Annie okay? How do I get her back?"

"Ain't going to happen tonight Connolly. These guys got some questions that need answers. If you don't have any that's your business. Somebody does. These guys will find out. I'll let you know tomorrow what I'm hearing."

CHAPTER 12

Finn sat on his bed and studied the box. It had some weird markings on it. He couldn't find any way to open it. Not that he really wanted to open it. But he felt compelled to try. Heck the guys wouldn't even touch it. *But it didn't really come from the grave did it? It came from the crate those men had put it in there. Didn't it?*

He put the box in his closet and went to the bathroom. Before he got into bed for the night he got the box out again. He tried again to open it and failed. Disappointed he put it back in his closet with his other junk that he never looked at anymore and went to bed.

When Finn woke he was standing by the back door in the kitchen in a cold sweat. He didn't know where he was at first. The dream faded. He was frightened but didn't know why. He could only remember someone shouting at him to step back from a bright ledge. He found his way back to bed and had disturbing dreams all night.

CHAPTER 13

Annie never could breathe very well through her nose, or at all sometimes of the year. Her mom said it was ragweed, but Dr. Goldstein had said it was dirty air from the furnace vents. Her parents changed out the coal furnace for an oil burner when she was still a child. That helped a little. Ragweed was still a problem, but right now it was the tape around her mouth.

She had calmed a little since they drove her to the warehouse. She caught a glimpse of her Dad there, although he did not see her in the back seat of the sedan. Now at least she knew why they had grabbed her off the street and tied her up. Same reason Jack got his ears burned. Something her Dad was being forced to do but was resisting. He'll do it now for sure, she hoped.

She studied her captives. The driver, who she could not see, chain smoked and had a nervous voice with an Irish accent. The woman who held her down in the back seat was probably early twenties. She was dressed like a slut and went heavy on the mascara. She talked too much even though the guy kept telling her to shut up. Annie got the idea that she, if not both of them, lived in Quincy. Now that she had lit up, the amount of smoke in the car was suffocating Annie.

"I think she's having trouble breathing. Maybe you should loosen the tape?" the woman said.

"Soon as I find a quiet place to pull over."

Mostly they had kept her head down on the back seat but now that she was struggling the woman beside her allowed her to sit up. Annie took note of road signage and visual clues to their locale.

The driver, a thin ugly man, parked at a turnout and removed the tape from her head and mouth.

"Shout and I'll hurt you," he said.

Shouting didn't occur to her, but she did bite his hand. Hard. She could taste his blood. He slugged her.

*

The skinny guy emerged from the Norfolk Tavern and got in a black sedan. Joe began tailing him. Joe knew he was good at surveillance but couldn't remember why. This guy was evil. Joe believed he had accepted a mission of stopping him from doing anymore harm. When he saw they had that girl from his house with them he became resolute. He couldn't remember who had given him the mission but he knew he was good at missions.

He'd tailed them all afternoon and evening around town. They headed down the South Shore past

Weymouth. It was getting late. Joe was getting weary. Somewhere around Hanover he lost the black sedan. He started losing his resolve but kept heading south. Soon he forgot all about the sedan and his mission.

What was I doing? Where was I going? There was a girl. At the house. That's it. I used to see her at the beach dances. We were going to the beach. See the fireflies at the marsh.

The waterfront facades were comfortably familiar to Joe. Hassad's Bar and Grille, the Brant Rock Fish Market, the neon Bowling sign, Este's Candy Kitchen guided him along to where he parked facing the ocean staring at Brant Rock itself.

He lost himself in the crashing waves for a long while before he started the engine and resumed following the coast. The land soon ended at a point occupied by a trailer park. He drove past an unattended kiosk and a sign with instructions about self-registering. Aware of neither, nor of the empty numbered campsites he passed, he pulled into a particular vacant site with the certainty of one who had come here many times before. It was Labor Day and the summer crowds had all marched home having declared summer over, however artificially. For Joe it was still summer. He felt like he had just come back from somewhere else, to a place where someone watched over him. His eyes itched so he rubbed them. He parked the truck and got out. The salt air and marsh scent flowed through his nostrils and filled his being. Breathing deeply he climbed into his camper bed.

"Good to be back," he said aloud, running his hand through his wavy gray mane he fell happily and soundly to sleep.

*

Joe woke up again. Something had awakened him earlier and he tried to remember what had occurred before he had fallen back asleep.

Something about a water faucet. Was it a dream?

He fumbled through a cabinet until he came up with a hefty black metal tube that was as much a club as it was a flashlight and climbed back into bed. He put his slacks and socks on. He pulled a dark hooded sweatshirt over his head. Grabbing the flashlight he lay down on top of the bed covers. He stared at the ceiling.

Now he remembered. He had awakened to the sound of a vehicle and looked out the window to see a car driving slowly around the campground loops.

Was it a dream? No.

"They'll come back," he said.

Having remembered he now felt calm. He'd been trained after all.

How? Soldier? Police? When? Didn't matter.

"Mind and body are one," he said quietly. He studied the skylight vent. He got up and opened it. He lay back down and stared through the vent at the stars. He had no thoughts. He felt calm, patient. He waited.

*

They're back. Joe recognized the sound of the approaching vehicle. He pulled up his sweatshirt hood. Holding the flashlight he climbed through the roof vent. He lay flat on his belly so he could peer over the side of the camper shell.

The driver stopped several campsites away and killed the engine. As the guy stepped out Joe caught a glimpse of a pistol in his boney right hand. The skinny guy headed straight for the camper shell door and pounded on it.

"Open up" he demanded. "Police. Open the door."

Joe stood up on the roof above the door. Much as he would like to use the flashlight as a weapon, he knew that it was a distraction that he needed most, so he threw it into the darkness. As the flashlight landed with a loud clunk Joe dropped down on the man, his hands encasing the man's right hand and gun. The pressure Joe applied to the wrist loosened the man's grip. The gun fell to the pavement and Joe kicked it away as he cupped the man's cranium and chin. With a quick twist he snapped his neck.

The car sped away as Joe stepped over the dead man and retrieved the flashlight. He got his shoes and keys out of the camper. It was quiet. There was no one in sight. He looked up at the stars for a few minutes. Then he got in the truck and drove away.

Later, as he was parked listening to the waves slapping in the darkness against Brant Rock, the calmness, the caution, the feelings of youth and summertime all rolled together and then away, and all he felt was lost.

CHAPTER 14

Lisa Ciccone knew she was in over her head. She couldn't think straight. She eased up on the gas pedal when she saw the Quincy sign and tried to focus. Should she take the girl to the apartment? How would she get her in there without the neighbors noticing. Maybe she should just drop her off somewhere in Dorchester and let her walk home.

"Let me go and I won't tell anyone about you."

Lisa looked to the back seat and saw that Annie was still tied up but somehow rubbed the gag free of her mouth.

"Fuck. How 'd you get that gag off your mouth?"

"He saw me you know. That's right. He saw me. And you. You better let me go. Cops will be looking for you. My father was a cop. He'll be coming for me."

Lisa pulled into the parking lot of a closed restaurant and stopped. She got out and went to the back. Annie struggled to keep from being gagged again. Lisa hit her.

"I can't stand the gag. I'll be quiet. No gag. Please?" Annie cried but to no avail and the gag was firmly replaced.

"Listen I don't know nothing about you. I was in the car to help my guy out with a job. Then we pick up these two guys and they have me bait you to the car so they could grab you. You know the rest. Now I'm a kidnapper and everyone else has split and I don't even know who they are or where to find them. So what the fuck am I supposed to do with you?"

She looked at Annie. Not as if she was expecting an answer. Annie could see it in her eyes. Eyes that had lost the ability to see any good in the world. Eyes that meant her only harm.

*

Joe opened his eyes to the sunrise. Cold and confused he searched the glove box unsure what he was looking for. When he came across a slip of paper with a phone number on it he paused.

My son? My sister? I could call someone.

The thought calmed him. He put the paper away and started the truck. A short while later he came across an intersection with Route 3A and a choice. Plymouth or Hanover Center. He chose Hanover. He passed familiar sights: Tedeschi's Market, Sumore Hamburgers, miniature golf. He got all the way to Milton before becoming disoriented. He parked and stood at Lower Mills bridge. The air was rich with the aroma of Baker's Chocolate roasting in the adjacent factory. Joe's mind flooded with memories from childhood. He stood there daydreaming for a very long time. Abruptly an image of a skinny guy, sprawled on the pavement with a broken neck, appeared in front of him like an hallucination. Then, in a rare moment of clarity, Joe decided to call home.

*

Lisa decided to risk bringing Annie to the apartment. If somebody saw her she'd just flee. After all it wasn't her place and no one could trace it to her. She got a sharp knife from the kitchen and untied Annie's legs. She had little trouble prodding her up the stairs. As best she could tell they went unnoticed.

In the bedroom she held the knife against Annie's throat and briefly considered killing her but didn't because she needed more time to think. Instead she rebound her legs and shoved her in the closet.

She lit a smoke and went back out as the sun was rising.

*

The phone rang. His Aunt Noreen was preoccupied with the cops in the kitchen so Mike picked it up and said hello.

"Who's this?" Joe said.

"Dad! Its Dad," he shouted into the phone and to those in the kitchen. "Where are you?"

"In a phone booth. Chocolate everywhere."

"He's at a payphone. Maybe near Baker's Mill. Says he smells chocolate," Mike relayed.

"We'll get a car moving through Lower Mills right away," said one of the cops. "And we'll head over there right now ourselves. Try to keep him on the line so he doesn't wander."

Mike heard the phone on the other end hang up.

CHAPTER 15

The two thugs stood uncomfortably in the back room Herky Sullivan called his office.

"You wanted to see us, Sully?" the guy in charge said.

"Sit down."

Sullivan was one of Jimmy's main guys and he was either going to pass along some orders to the two nervous foot soldiers or have them taken out for a ride.

Everyone called him Herky. It was short for Hercules, whom the wimpy looking Sully did not resemble. They only called him Sully to his face.

"So we got the dope deal misunderstanding straightened out. You guys are off the hook. But Jimmy wants you to clean the slate. Start with Fat Eddie before the cops get to him. Then find Hanna, that Ciccone bitch, and the Connolly girl. This has been such a fuck up. Only way to fix it is to wipe it all clean. Ya got it?"

The two relieved thugs nodded that they did, and left.

Sullivan eased back in his chair, lit a smoke and gathered his thoughts. It had been a rough night. The dumb fuck plant inside the museum thought he could get away with switching out the dope stash and unloading it from a safe haven. He was a dead man anyway because he knew too much. In the perverse way his sociopathic mind worked Sullivan felt justified that the guy died thinking it was because he screwed up. And these two dumb fucks. Soon as they do the clean up work he'd put out a contract to have them hit. Clean slate. Just him and Jimmy. This last thought gave Sullivan pause. He wondered if Jimmy called him Herky behind his back.

*

"Fat Eddie Mahoney's dead. Shot in the head and dumped down by Florian Hall. Must have happened right after you spoke with him last night."

The detectives were seated in the Connolly parlor. Frank held is arms around his wife, who for the moment was not hysterical.

"It was good that you called us right away. As you know Frank, the first few hours are critical in these cases."

"These cases! Cases! What cases? We're talking about my daughter here," Irene Connolly practically screamed.

"The best chance of getting your daughter back safely is in the first twenty-four hours. We are in that window and doing everything we can Mrs. Connolly." The beefy detective named Rogers spoke calmly, then looked at Frank. "It's unfortunate that we didn't get a chance to talk with Mahoney. Is there anything you didn't tell us about your conversation at the bar Frank?"

"You guys got it all. Wasn't much."

"Okay, then how about at the warehouse. You be able to recognize anyone if we put them in a lineup?"

"The driver, yeah. Looked like a scarecrow. The other guys had their faces covered. Might recognize their eyes, but it was dark. Mostly I was looking at the barrel of the gun. You know?"

"Alright then," "We'll have a composite guy come right over. He'll sketch this driver for you. We'll also get a sketch from your boy on the two punks that burned his ears. When we find them I expect they'll lead us uselessly back to Mahoney. So if you can think of anything else…"

Rogers and his much smaller partner stood. The smaller detective hesitated at the door.

"We'll find your Annie," he said looking directly at Irene Connolly.

Good cop bad cop routine, thought Frank, feeling like a suspect.

*

Lisa Ciccone knew that the Norfolk Tavern in Dorchester was a place that Hanna frequented. She drove there hoping that she might recognize someone. Anyone related to all this so she could arrange to unload the girl.

The place looked like it was closed. But the door opened and several men slipped out from the cavernous dark and into the morning light. She recognized two of the them from last night. She could see that one guy recognized her. Before she could exit he opened the passenger door and slid in beside her. Another guy got in the back and pressed a gun behind her head.

"Drive," the guy beside her said.

CHAPTER 16

Mike dropped the blood-stained pink sweater into the evidence bag Detective Rogers held open. Joe Scanlon said he'd found it in the camper. Mike identified it as the sweater Annie was wearing when last seen.

The detectives weren't having any more success than he or his aunt had questioning Joe.

"Okay Joe, think again how you came across this sweater. Where you went. What you were doing," Rogers inquired.

"Lady by a water faucet. Pushy, she … ," he looked at his sister and trailed off, looking embarrassed.

"And? What she do?" Rogers pressed but Joe fell silent.

"What she look like?"

"Who?" Joe said.

The smaller detective let out a chuckle that obviously irritated Rogers.

"Sorry," he said. "Who's on first? You know?"

Rogers gave up and addressed Joe's sister.

"Here's what we got. Neighbor lady named Mrs. Steinman is the last person we know to see Annie Connolly. Out front here, she says, with Joe's arm around Annie and him saying they're going to the beach. Next, according to Frank Connolly, she's taken hostage so he'll let them have access to a museum warehouse. According to the museum a trunk was taken from the warehouse last night. This morning a caretaker at the Codman graveyard picking up litter finds a tomb vandalized and sees a trunk inside. Museum officials identify it as the one stolen. They say it contains African or Haitian items, probably worthless, recently donated by a neighborhood guy who's having his cousin committed. Now, Joe shows up here with the girl's bloody sweater. Oh yeah, and the only person who could tell us more other than Joe is a fat loan shark at the morgue with a hole in his head."

"So you're saying Joe's a suspect?" said an appalled Noreen Scanlon. "What about Frank Connolly? He's a drinker and a gambler. He wouldn't hurt his own daughter I know, but something could have gone wrong. Maybe he knows more than he's letting on."

"Oh Joe's a suspect alright. I think maybe he knows more than he's letting on. Taking him in at this point would probably do more harm than good. Keep talking to him. Call me if you find out anything new. And let me worry about Frank Connolly."

The detectives headed for the door. Mike was out well before them.

*

"Shouldn't you give them the box, Finn?" Mike said.

"What and have them haul me into juvie as a grave robber? Besides you said they called it a crazy lady's junk. I'll bet it belonged to the old witch. I'm keeping it man."

"But what if it somehow could help find Annie?" Tony chimed in from his perch on the schoolyard fire escape.

"No way a dusty old box can do that. But you know that skinny kid from juvie I told you about. I bet he knows where she is," Finn said.

"What skinny kid?" Mike said.

"The one that Tony here said was asking about Darlington Street. The one with the creepy little brother."

"Sounds like the guys I chased away from little Jack when they were burning his ears," Mike said.

"Just putting two and two together. So why we wasting time here? I know where they hang out at the projects," Finn said.

*

Finn led his friends into the maze of identical brick boxes that everyone called the Franklin Field Projects, although the vandalized signage identified it as some variation of the Boston Housing Authority. If you lived there it was simply "the projects". If you were lucky, you didn't live there very long.

At juvie Finn said the skinny kid, Hanna, told him a bit about the projects when he wasn't violently acting up. Finn told him that he had lived there for a few years with his mother. Hanna said his mother still lived there and his father shared custody for them in Quincy. Finn guessed that since Hanna and his brother had started coming around the neighborhood, they were probably visiting with the mother. From Hanna's description, he even knew which building. It was the same one Finn had lived in years before.

Mike was tense and hyper alert as they moved through the alleys. Tony was justifiably petrified, as this was "white only" turf. The city had constructed "black only" projects elsewhere. Finn was calm. He was in fight mode. Looking to do some good for his friends the only way he knew how.

They didn't have to travel far. Hanna came around a corner alone and unaware. They surrounded him.

"Too fuckin' chicken to go one on one, huh?" he said looking squarely at Finn.

"I can take him," Finn said.

"Nope. He's mine," Mike said as he let a left hook fly.

Hanna stepped to the side and kicked Mike squarely in the balls.

Tony started to move toward Hanna as Mike crumpled to the ground.

"C'mon nigga," Hanna said laughing.

"My turn Tony," Finn said.

Hanna couldn't side-step Finn's one-two. The third punch ended it. Hanna immediately became submissive, as is always the way with bullies.

*

The skinny kid's name was Henry Hanna, but he preferred "Butch". He blabbed incessantly as they made their way quickly out of the projects across the tracks and up Southern Avenue to the school yard. He said his Dad came from Ireland looking for a cousin who supposedly was a big shot at the chocolate mill but it all turned out to be just a story. After his little brother was born his father split and took a job in Quincy which he lost and now, according to his mother, was just 'a no good thieving pimp.' He told them how they hurt Jack Connolly because of this guy at the liquor store. But when he paid them the next day their father just happened to be at the store. It turned out he knew this guy and the two got to talking about a job to do. They told Butch and his brother to get lost.

"The job your father and this guy were talking about have anything to do with the father of the kid you hurt?" Mike said.

"Probably," Butch replied.

"You know where your Dad's place is in Quincy?" Tony said.

"Sure. Me and my brother go there a lot. Three eighty-six Main Street apartment number twelve. Key is hidden above the door. If my old man is home his black Buick will be out front."

"C'mon let's go," said Finn.

"Huh?" Mike said.

"Pooey won't miss his car for awhile. We're going to Quincy," Finn said.

CHAPTER 17

At daybreak Marshfield cops found a John Doe dead of a broken neck on the pavement of a trailer park in Brant Rock. Later that day one of the town cops saw a resemblance to the composite Rodgers had posted on the noon TV news. They delivered Rodgers a morgue photo. He showed it to Frank Connolly who identified the Marshfield body as the driver of the vehicle at the warehouse. The fingerprints brought a match to a Michael Hanna out of Quincy who had a rap sheet for running prostitutes and drugs. Quincy Police checked the last known address, which turned out to be a vacant house in Houghs Neck.

Rogers and his partner were pondering these developments as they stood over the body of a twenty-three year old prostitute that turned up in an alley near Franklin Field with multiple bullet wounds. Lisa Ciccone's rap sheet linked her to Hanna through prostitution convictions.

"Assuming she was on the kidnapping with Hanna, how does she end up here while he gets dropped in Marshfield?" Rogers wondered.

"And where does that leave the Connolly girl?" his partner added.

"Exactly," Rogers said. "C'mon let's go get some coffee. My head hurts."

They drove along Talbot Avenue toward Dunkin Donuts. They passed Butch walking along the sidewalk. Rogers studied his face as they passed.

"Turn us around," he told his partner. "He's the kid in the sketch."

*

It took Finn less than a minute to hot wire Pooey's Plymouth Valiant. His friends had no idea where he learned this skill. They never participated in any of his joy rides. This time was different. They had a destination and a purpose that justified Finn's action. They hoped Pooey would understand. Mike knew the way to Quincy. Their new "pal" Butch wanted to come with them but they told him to get lost.

Finn parked Pooey's car on Main Street in Quincy and grabbed the tire iron that was on the back seat floor. They climbed the stairs to the second floor unit where Mike located the key above the moulding. There was no Buick out front so there was no need to be cautious.

The apartment door locking automatically behind them was the only sound. It was quiet inside. So quiet that when they all stopped moving about they could her muffled cries from the bedroom closet. So quiet they could hear footsteps coming up the stairs.

*

With no way out the boys tried to melt into the walls. Tony and Mike stood beside the entry door so that they would be hidden when it opened. Finn ducked into the small adjacent kitchen space.

Someone pounded on the door. Twice. The third time was more than a knock. The door flew open and two men moved in. The first moved toward the bedroom in the rear. The other moved to the side near the kitchen and bathroom. The refrigerator jutted out just enough for Finn to conceal himself as the second man moved past him and toward the bathroom.

"Clear," he said.

"Bedroom is clear," said the guy in charge. "Quiet. Listen. You hear that? She's in the closet," he said.

Some skills not taught in school needed to be learned on the streets of Codman Square. Assessing threat is one of the required skills. Dealing with it is another. Each boy knew that these men were not here to help Annie, and that they had to act.

Finn moved quickly from the kitchen and fiercely struck the unsuspecting second guy on the head with the tire iron. Tony and Mike rushed forward to the bedroom. The first man moved back toward the commotion drawing a handgun from his jacket. He was about to fire it at Finn when Mike tackled him. Tony moved in and they all stumbled together. The guy got off two shots before Finn was able to knock the gun free.

One missed.

*

With the information Butch Hanna provided him, Detective Rogers alerted the Quincy Police and met them at the Main Street apartment. Their whole approach changed when they heard the shots.

Rogers, his partner, and the two Quincy cops all drew their weapons and hurried up the stairs. The Quincy cops went in first.

"Police. Don't anyone move," said the second cop in the door as the first covered the room with his weapon.

Tony put his hands in the air. Finn and the guy who fired the shots moved off each other and did the same.

"This kid needs an ambulance," Rogers said as he looked at Mike who was down and bleeding profusely from a head wound. "Check that guy down over there," Rogers said to his partner. "And cuff him."

Rogers picked the gun up off the floor as one of the officers cuffed the shooter.

"What are you two and young Scanlon doing here for chrissakes?" he said.

"Annie's in the bedroom closet," Finn answered.

"We came to get her," Tony said.

*

Rogers knew that the Quincy police had started hiring female traffic officers. He asked if one could be sent in to talk with Annie and comfort her in the apartment bedroom. Traffic Officer Darlene Winters promptly arrived, allowing Rodgers to help coordinate the crime scene.

"Annie this is Officer Winters. She's going to sit here with you for a bit while we get hold of your parents," Rogers told her.

"Hi Annie, you can call me Darlene okay? How are you feeling?"

"Better now that I can breathe and I'm not all tied up."

"Did they hurt you?"

"They hit me a couple of times. That's all."

"You sure that's all."

"Yeah, that's all. Is Mike okay?"

"Well he had to go to the hospital."

"He saved me didn't he?"

"Yes he saved you, sweetie. Now can you tell me what happened?"

"This woman asked me for directions. Then she pushed me into a guy who pulled me into a car. They tied me up and gagged me. Told me that my Dad needed to do what they wanted and I was like their insurance."

"Hold on a sec. Detective do you have any photos or composites?" Officer Winters called out to the front room.

Rogers brought in two booking photos and showed them to Annie.

"Is this the man and woman who did this to you?" he said.

"That's them. I think he's dead now."

"Yes he is. How do you know that?"

"I bit his hand and made him bleed."

"Good for you," said Officer Winters.

"No, that didn't kill him. It made him mad and he hit me. I kinda got knocked out and they took off my sweater because his blood was on it. He wanted her to wash it out. See when I came to they were talking about a truck following them. Then they pulled a trick somehow and ended up following the truck. The guy said he wanted to know who was driving it."

"Go on, tell us the whole story," said Rogers.

"So they followed the truck to a campground, and decided that the woman should try to lure the guy out. So she was washing the sweater at the water faucet by the truck and pretending to be getting water and a guy came out from the camper on the back. It was Mr. Scanlon. I know he saw me but they didn't notice. He went back in and we drove away. Only the guy was upset with her. He said she didn't set the guy up for him like he told her. She said Mr. Scanlon was retarded. She said she even offered to give Mr. Scanlon a ... give him sex, but he refused. Then she started swearing and said she left the sweater at the faucet."

"Did they go back for the sweater?"

"Yeah only this time the guy went to the truck with a gun. I couldn't really see but the woman panicked and drove us away. Later she said the guy was dead."

"And she brought you here."

"Yeah after she hit me again."

"Well it's all over now and you're safe. Your family is safe. They're going to meet you at the hospital where you're going to get checked out okay?"

"Same hospital as Mike?"

"Yeah, honey. Same place. Why?"

"Cause if I ever have to go to a hospital I want Mike there with me to hold my hand."

CHAPTER 18

"I'm sorry about your son Joe," Detective Rogers said.

"Why?" said Joe. "Where is he?"

"How is Mike doing, M'am?" Rogers said, turning to Mike's Aunt Noreen.

"He is still in emergency care. Day to day. We don't know. Just keep praying," she said.

"I wanted you to know that the Connolly girl explained Joe's part in this was heroic. At least the part that she knows. We can't figure out how he got involved at all. Seems mostly coincidental except the girl said that the kidnappers believed Joe was following them. But that was right after she got knocked unconscious and she was a little fuzzy on details."

Rogers turned back to Joe. "You remember following a black Buick down to the beach on your camping trip Joe?"

"No."

"We'd like to close the case on the death of the male kidnapper at the Brant Rock campsite but Annie didn't see anything from where the car was parked. Joe, you must have picked up the sweater from the ground where Annie said the woman suspect left it. Annie also said that the woman told her that you killed the guy. That true Joe? Can you tell me what happened?"

"A mission," Joe said. He looked away, clearly finished with discussion.

"Give me a call if he has anything to add," said Rogers turning his attention back to Joe's sister. "We're going to put it down as self-defense although the guy probably never saw it coming. Personally, I think Joe should get another medal."

CHAPTER 19

The thugs from the Quincy apartment gave up Herky Sullivan before being charged with kidnapping and attempted murder. The cops moved quickly but found Sullivan dead in his car. Execution style. Later they filed it as a cold case knowing full well the sudden proliferation of heroin throughout New England by the Irish mafia completed the story.

Tony received an admonishment from the juvenile court for riding in the stolen car, but the neighbors all treated him like a hero. Even Angelo Papoulias, who brought a jar of honey from his hive over to the house, put a good word in for him at the courthouse.

Finn didn't fare as well. The court was fed up with his habitual appearances. Given his heroics, and the fact his home situation was hopeless, the court and his probation officer took unusual steps in arranging placement for him in an experimental residential school program where he could learn a trade as well as become "reformed".

Mike never made it home from the hospital.

*

Baker's Chocolate closed the Lower Mills factory. Irene Connolly placed the items from her desk drawer into a bag and walked home from the Mill, her job ended. As she walked she became lost in thought. She never much liked the place anyway. Never would have even have been offered the job if it wasn't for Helen Scanlon and the nosy personnel lady at Baker's. Helen's maiden name was Hannan. The personnel lady had a hobby of tracing family histories and she connected Helen all the way back to a co-founder of Baker's named Hannan. She hired Helen immediately, and picked up Irene just because Helen asked.

Of course Helen died shortly after from the cancer, Irene remembered. Then Helen's husband started going soft in the head. And their son Mike off to the hospital with a bullet in his head. Terrible. So many troubles it seemed like the place operated under a curse. And of course there was the incident just before she started working there. A small plane full of Baker executives crashed in the Brazilian jungle while on a cacao bean purchasing trip. All were killed and the story shrouded in secrecy and conspiracy.

As she walked, she thought about the other changes in store. Her divorce from Frank was in the works, and she'd found a decent place to live down the South Shore with good schools for Annie and Jack.

Time to move on.

CHAPTER 20

**Transition Years
Codman Square
Dorchester**

It seemed to Tony that everyone moved away all at once. He knew that wasn't true because he'd watched it happen one family, one store front at a time now for two years. Last week Joe Scanlon's sister Noreen finally put him in a nursing home, and moved to Quincy. Yesterday Manny closed his barbershop after twenty years of providing mens and boys regulars, complete with bottles of Beau Junior hair slop. The fish market shut down.

He also knew that everyone wasn't going to move away. His family was staying put. Another way to look at it was that everyone is moving in all at once. Each day he watched a new family arrive to fill a recently vacated flat. Most were colored, some Haitian like him. As the cultural mix changed the businesses responded. Lena's Variety became a Kreyol market. Kaspar Brothers Market reopened as a Baptist church.

He made new friends. Graduated from Dorchester High School. Got a job driving a canteen truck while he tried getting on with the Boston Police Department.

Tony missed the scent of chocolate in the air.

NOW

CHAPTER 21

Sean Leahy was one of the small contingent of young Harvard educated professionals being groomed for executive and cabinet level positions in the City of Boston hierarchy. Most of his cohorts came from the business school. Sean's degree was in public policy and urban planning with emphasis on emergency response. Just thirty years old, many of the staff he led were old enough to be his parents. True to the nature of bureaucracies his title was easy to trip over. Deputy Chief of the Boston Police Department Regional Intelligence Center.

He shut down the alarm sounding from his phone and quickly rose. It was the third alarm. The late night celebration of his father's sixtieth birthday would cost him his casual breakfast routine. But he didn't regret it. They had a great time, starting and ending at the Eire Pub with Fenway in between. But now he'd have to get in gear if he was going to make the President's appearance on time.

He scooped up the Boston Globe from his North End doorstep and hustled over to the subway. As he walked he thought of how different he was than his father. About the only things they had in common were strong wrists, ham hock hands and rugged Irish good looks. Finn Leahy had always been in trouble growing up while Sean rarely did anything wrong. But Sean liked trouble. Facing it. Not making it. He figured that also made him like Finn only from the other side of a thin blue line. He signed on as Patrolman the week after he graduated from college. He skyrocketed to Lieutenant. A sabbatical to attend the Kennedy School at Harvard resulted in the Mayor creating a special liaison position for him as the highest ranking commissioned officer at the Intelligence Center. His position gave him broad powers in Incident Command situations.

He decided to make up some time by jumping off the T at Shawmut, instead of staying on one more stop until Ashmont and taking the bus transfer to Codman Square. Of course he could have taken a city car, or had an officer drive him. Sean like to ride the transit whenever possible. He felt it kept him in touch with the people, his roots. He hoofed it up the hill on Centre Street. It was a smart move because he could sense by the tension in the crowd that the President's appearance was imminent.

Sean worked his way through a gap on the right side of the crowd, then through another as he angled toward the stage. He had no official role this close in. The Boston Police had staged under his team's direction outside this perimeter, within which it was all Secret Service. Sean could easily have got himself positioned backstage with them but he wanted to see the whole picture of how they shielded the man in such an exposed setting. He also wanted to see and hear President Obama's delivery.

"You can't go past here," said the attractive young black woman wearing a Health Center vest and blocking his way.

"Oh sorry," said Sean, noticing that the woman was one of several Health Center staff forming a human barrier.

"Staff only beyond this point," she said.

"Not a problem. I'm good right here," he said as he took full appraisal of her, noticing that she was doing the same to him.

"Do you enjoy your work here?" he said, making small talk.

"I better because I sure don't do it for the pay." After a pause she said, "I volunteer a few hours each week."

"That's admirable," he said, shooting her an admiring look.

"How about you," she said, warming. "What do you do when you're not trying to push your way through a crowd?"

"I think I pushed to a good spot don't you?" he said nodding toward the stage but clearly meaning something else. "I work for the City," he said handing her his card.

"How about you? What do you do when you're not voluntarily confronting aggressive men?"

"I'm a nurse, but these days mostly I'm doing graduate study in Public Health at Harvard."

Sean read the card she handed him.

"Ketia Depestre. Talbot Institute? The place has been in the news lately hasn't it?"

"If you call what the Herald prints news, then yes. There's been a reporter trying to create a stir."

A pulse went through the crowd and the ambient noise level rose several decibels.

The President of the United States was welcomed. Sean's attention became divided.

CHAPTER 22

As an expert on recurring dreams it never ceased to amaze Harvard Professor Melissa White how inept she was at interpreting her own. A Tarot card reader in a public square could do better. As she woke she struggled to remember any details beyond a vaguely familiar girl and an ubiquitous sense of urgency to contact her. Coming into focus in her periphery was an alarm clock threatening to herald a new day. Melissa quickly shut it down and headed to the bathroom.

Her shower thoughts morphed from her dream to the lecture she would give later this morning in her *Quantum Perspective in Dream Psychology* class. In a nearly thirty-year tenure she had never taught a class so popular, or controversial.

An accomplished physicist, Melissa White had muddied academic waters when she crossed over to the psychology department stretching theoretical strings into the behavioral realm. Popular with students and an attentive media, mainstream academia had little patience with her subject matter. The publish or perish mantra bequeathed her little more than another semester on this side of the river unless she produced some remarkable results.

Nonetheless the premise was enchanting. She presented the students an intriguing hypothesis that each living being was physically connected, not only in the present, but also throughout the past and future. Drawing from contemporary physics she challenged her students to study these connections, using an unusual toolbox of history and dreams. The foundation of the theory being that the two realms were both equally reliable. History being no more or less real than a dream. She demonstrated to her psychology students how physicists similarly measured space and time with about the same level of confidence, yet without considering human consciousness. Perhaps (and this was her hook) a mathematics of physics cannot be completely understood without a toolbox developed from psychological research. In her lab the dreaming brain stood in for the cosmos.

By the time she turned off the shower, her dream was gone as well as any connection to her morning lecture. There was a time this would have frustrated her. Now she simply accepted that while one had happened and the other yet to come, both events remain simultaneously linked in her mind. What she did not remember, she also did not forget. At least in theory.

Freshened with coffee in hand she made her way to the Harvard Square T station, and the redline train that carried her to a morning meeting at Mass General Hospital with Michael Meacham, her research partner, and the graduate assistants they supervised.

In transit Professor White remembered that there would be a new subject processed into their study today, a comatose woman about her age with an inoperable brain tumor. By the terms of the signed agreements, her brain would become property of the hospital after her death, and the Harvard research group to which Meacham belonged would have access to it for their specified purposes.

White exited the T at Charles Street and walked the short distance to the main lobby of MGH where she met her students. Hastened but cordial greetings preceded an elevator ride to the 15th floor where the new subject lay immobile in a private room.

*

Dr. Michael Meacham was an early riser. Most of his neighbor commuters were still sleeping soundly when he arrived at the Talbot Institute in Quincy for his morning rounds. His routine was to finish at the Institute around nine and drive the Expressway to Boston as the traffic flow lightened up. He enjoyed his work at MGH and was looking forward to his meeting this morning with Melissa White and their new patient. But his true passion was his work at the Institute and the patients who resided there.

Talbot was a completely unique entity. The patients, called residents, were there for life. New applicants were rarely admitted to the 12-room facility.

To the neighboring community Talbot appeared as a convalescent home for the extremely wealthy. Its prominent architecture and well-landscaped grounds were considered an enhancement to property values, as well as a boon to the tax base. Little else was ever considered, so to some Talbot seemed mysterious. Technically in Quincy, the facility stood on a landfill a mere stone's throw across the Neponset River from the Dorchester neighborhood called Port Norfolk.

Meacham and White were able to establish the Institute through the beneficence of old money from families whose relatives were accepted as residents. The endowment from these six families allowed for the admission of six additional residents, each of who had unique brain disorders. All six had been diagnosed with dementia. Three were comatose. While White studied the relationship of dreams with dementia, hypnosis and other states, Meacham was expert at inducing and relieving coma. He had many interests. Talbot was his lab. The patients were his rats.

*

Drs. Meacham and White finished examining the new patient, a sixty-year old comatose woman with long gray hair and a girlish face named Ann

Winston. When they quizzed the interns for observations, none could offer any comments better than unremarkable, so they were sent off to their next assignment.

Over coffee in the MGH cafeteria Melissa White said, "How did the morning go at Talbot, Michael? You look uncharacteristically melancholy." What she really meant was that her pale gaunt colleague looked more melancholy than usual. White kept herself tanned and fit. She thought Meacham to be unhealthy.

"I'm sorry to have to tell you that Arthur Ludlow died in his sleep early this morning," Meacham said.

"I am sorry to hear that. Has the family been notified?"

"Not just yet."

"Michael why not?

"Because we both know quite well that the revenue stream to the endowment from the Ludlow trust ceases upon Arthur's death. I haven't pronounced him. I gave staff strict orders to stay out of his room until we get there, unless summoned. He flat lined. Of course there is brain death but I kept the organs on life support. We could simulate a coma, buy some time, maybe the lawyers could renegotiate the trust?"

"You what? I'm sorry but that is completely unacceptable. Surely you see the risk is just too great, Michael. We've got to accept the loss, adjust the budget, and move on."

"You know there are no resident applicants currently on the short list. These hard times have caused even the wealthiest to scale back."

"The way I see it we have an open bed, albeit unfunded, to bring on a new resident subject. The interns didn't catch it, but we know Ann Winston is anything but unremarkable. We could speak to the family about her long-term care needs. Get them to take a look at Talbot and consider their options. When they appreciate that it will cost them nothing, I'm sure they'll sign whatever we present."

"I guess that probably is our best option."

"Then you'll head back and take care of Ludlow?"

"I'm on my way. Oh, there's one more thing I must tell you Melissa."

"You've had quite a morning, huh?"

"No, no wait, this is a surprise you won't mind hearing. Sam Stockton woke up this morning for about ten minutes."

"Outstanding!"

"Better still. He spoke. Check the transcripts. You'll be pleased."

CHAPTER 23

The woman saw the fear in their dark faces had not lessened. Their bodies still trembled. The mother hugged her son tightly. The boy was perhaps twelve and he could not speak.

"There is little more I can do," the woman said, as she blew out the candles on the small altar. They were able to communicate in Kreyol better than English, although it was clearly not the mother's native tongue.

"He spoke just fine until trances came. Now he is silent and often walks like the dead. Please help us," the mother said.

The woman said nothing but accepted a piece of paper from the young mother.

"New England Avenue?" the woman read aloud.

"It is where they brought us," the mother said.

"For the time being you will stay here with me."

*

It was one of Sergeant Tony Sebastiene's two off-duty days from the force, which weren't exactly the same as days off because he often got called in, or signed on for police overtime detail. Otherwise, like today, he worked a semi-regular afternoon shift at his second job, security at the Codman Square Health Center.

The Great Hall housed the Health Center executive offices and was among the top three prominent buildings comprising Codman Square.

Tony thought most would agree the Reverend Codman's historic white Congregational Church holds center court. The Boston Latin Academy building, originally Dorchester High School, now converted to apartments garners second place. The Health Center office building gets third among several other impressive historic structures nearby. Tony remembered going to the Hall as a child when it was the Public Library. Originally it was the site of the Dorchester Town Hall. Somewhere in this triangulation he knew Baker's General Store and residence once existed.

Tony stood near the front door to the Center as a deterrent to trouble and a symbol of safety. That was his main duty. One that many would find monotonous. Not so Tony. He had a kind word or pleasant observation for everyone within earshot. Such was his gregarious nature. When foot traffic was slow, as it was now, he stared out at the intersection. In his mind he would imagine how it was in the eighteenth century.

Sometimes he would remember how it looked when he was a kid. Hot summer days were best. Scrape together some change and buy a lime rickey at the corner shop. If you had any coins left you could pool them with Mike and Finn and go to the Smoke Shop on Talbot Avenue where they sold all kinds of gags and mischievous items. Their favorite purchase was a three pack of stink bombs. Glass capsules filled with sulfuric rotten egg concentrate. Thank God they banned those, Tony thought. His cop job was hectic enough without having to deal with calls from local merchants or tenants whose entire stores and three decker houses were cleared for hours by a kid who crushed one of those things near the store dairy counter, or inside the decker foyer.

    Tony thought of Mike and Finn. Seemed like that whole world, their universe really, came to a violent end as that summer in 1965 came to a close. That was truly it for Mike, but whatever became of Finn? Tony vaguely remembered him kicking around for a month or two when he got back from his vocational training. Then came the court-ordered school integration, the forced busing. Fear, violence, retaliation, more violence. Years later a resurgence of community focus took hold in the eighties with the Health Center a focal point. Tony guessed it served about twenty thousand patients every year, most well below poverty with annual incomes around four grand. Violence persists. Poverty. Violence. Chicken or egg?

    "Day trippin' Tony?"

    "Hello Ketia. How are you this fine day? Yeah, I was spaced there a bit."

    "I noticed. Thanks. I'm just fine. Ready to do a shift with the people. Bring them on."

    Ketia slipped through the doors leaving Tony with his day dreams. *She's a fine lady,* he thought. *About the same age as Christian.* From what he could draw out of her, he believed she was single. Like his son Chris, she was born into the neighborhood from Haitian parents. An introduction was in order.

*

Edmund White poured his wife two fingers of Glenlivet over ice with a splash. He took his neat and handed her the tumbler before sitting in the soft chair adjacent to hers in their parlor. This was their pre-dinner ritual most nights, an intellectual sparring match they both enjoyed. His work as a trust attorney was lucrative but boring compared to Melissa's classroom and research. Smothered daily by credential seekers and sycophants, she found her nightly conservative challenges reliably refreshing.

"Find any elusive particles or chinks in the space-time continuum today sweetheart?" he said.

"Well, brace yourself hon, the answer is yes actually."

"Really?"

"Michael got Sam Stockton on record today."

"That's amazing. He hasn't checked in for what five, six months?"

"Closer to eight."

"And?"

"Well the most recent scenario we'd given him focused on the Revolutionary War. His dream report was clearly 1775, but except for a reference to the Battle of Dorchester Heights, he spoke mostly of comings and goings surrounding a place called the Liberty Tree Tavern."

"Was there such a place?"

"Right on the mark. Colonel Lemuel Robinson, Proprietor."

"I assume the Colonel was referenced in the scenarios."

"Oh yes. He led the Patriots to victory at the Heights. But we knew nothing of the tavern until Stockton spoke of it."

"I'd double check the scenario input if I were you."

"Done that. Nothing there."

"Still you can't rule out the possibility that Stockton previously acquired life memory of the tavern."

"Not yet, but we will."

"And that will prove exactly what?"

"Well you know it won't prove anything. You asked about chinks. I'll add it to my list of chinks. Now how was your day in the world of legal finances."

"Exciting as ever. I moved another chunk of trust money into another chunk pile."

"Ha ha. Speaking of trusts. Arthur Ludlow died this morning."

"Whoa. Quite a day. I bet that dries up a significant revenue stream."

"But wait. Michael actually proposed keeping the trust intact by not pronouncing Ludlow."

"What?"

"Simulate coma or some such nonsense. I told him no way. He may be brilliant, but I have no idea how he passed his ethics classes in med school."

"How do you simulate a coma on someone who is deceased? Never mind. The man is a snake. Be careful Melissa. Stay the course with your research. Keep yourself clear of Michael Meacham's machinations, especially the financials. We've talked about this before."

"Yes counselor we have. And again, you are absolutely correct."

*

Finn stood groggily in the bathroom. It took him a moment to recognize the owner of the eyes staring at him. A long terrifying moment. He was looking at himself in the mirror. He'd been dreaming. Sleepwalking. His t-shirt and boxers were soaked with clammy sweat. He splashed some water on his face and went to the kitchen to get some coffee going.

Last night he went to the Sox game with Sean. They went to the Eire but he didn't get drunk. What else? He couldn't think straight. Then it came to him. When they walked by Cedar Grove Cemetery on the way to the trolley he'd remembered the time he went into Codman's tomb. He'd mentioned it to Sean. And when he came home last night he dug out the old box for some reason. Until yesterday it had been years since he thought of it. Now the dream and the sleepwalking are back. It was because he'd been handling the box again. He was sure of it. Wasn't he in denial about any cause and effect when he stashed it away all those years ago? Still, it's just a box. But he did stash it away. He felt sick to his stomach. Confused. Trapped. How to fight this? Where to run?

Something, some voice was in his head. He wondered if this is what Alzheimer's feels like. Mostly Finn felt lost, and he didn't like it.

Her last client of the day was an eleven year old with anger issues. His mother accompanied him. The purpose of the visit was to obtain refills on the several medications he had been prescribed since he was six. Ketia processed the prescriptions after engaging the boy a bit, and quizzing the mother about his recent range of behavior. The consultation left her feeling down as she ended her shift. Would we ever get past trying to medicate the anger of poverty and deal with the root problems? She thought the Health Center was a good starting place for creating a culture of community well-being but knew it was not enough. She volunteered here to make a difference, to give back to the neighborhood where she was born. She finished up her day with some boring paperwork at the administrative office. She headed out the door feeling ineffective.

"Have a good evening Ms. Ketia," said a cheerful Tony, lifting her spirit already.

"You as well, Tony. This must be your son?" she said, noting the handsome man with smiling facial features that mirrored Tony.

"Chris Sebastiene, Anchante! Koman ou ye?" said Tony's son, extending his hand as there was no need for Tony to acknowledge the obvious.

"Ketia Depestre. Tou al byen. Thank you. I've heard much about you from your father. Pleasure to finally meet you. I've never heard your father speak a word of Kreyol."

"He picked that up from his mother," Tony said. "Chris and I are going to walk down Norfolk to the Taste for a bite. Care to join us?"

"Love the jerk chicken there, but no thanks. Sorry. I have a date. Another time?" Ketia said, noting the disappointment expressed identically on the two faces. "Do you have a card?" she said, looking at Chris.

"I, ah, I'm between jobs," Chris stumbled.

"Oh well that seems to be going around. I hear you are a computer wiz. You'll find something soon. Here's my card. Talbot Institute. Call the number and ask for Melissa White. Tell her I referred you. I think she's looking for someone with your skills to help with their research."

"Thank you, I will do that. Enjoy your evening," Chris said.

"You too, orevwa," Ketia said as she departed.

"You said she was unattached," Chris said.

"Who says she's not. I said she was single. Call her."

CHAPTER 24

Sean only had enough time to check some of his e-mails while grabbing a coffee at the café on the North End side street where he lived alone in a small apartment. He moved quickly along the narrow streets of the old neighborhood across the Greenway and through the Haymarket. He was headed to the FBI headquarters at Government Center. The Special Agent in Charge asked him to meet with the local State Department liaison for a sensitive briefing. As usual he was running late.

He skipped right on by his office at City Hall, crossed the plaza and rode a crowded elevator to the FBI reception desk. He was buzzed through and escorted to a small conference room by a pleasant woman who offered him a much-needed second cup of coffee.

Special Agent Neil Bersconi entered shortly and introduced Paul Stearns from State, and Suzanne Sanchez from Massachusetts Homeland Security who both entered with him. Sean had met the burly FBI agent before. In fact Bersconi had relatives that were neighbors of Sean in the Italian enclave of Boston that defined the North End. He quickly sized up the two newcomers. Stearns struck him as weak and ineffectual with his tepid handshake and small pasty countenance. Sanchez came across just the opposite. A tall strong-boned woman with a firm grip and a steady eye. Sean noted the resemblance to J.Lo. They all exchanged pleasantries. Then Bersconi took charge.

"While our investigation is in its preliminary stages and our information is sketchy, Paul and I believe we need to prepare for the possibility of an act of terrorism involving biological weapons. State Department has information that a terrorist network is operating within the City's Haitian community. We have an agent deep in the Dorchester community. Indications are that persons unknown are arranging purchase of humans to carry out suicide missions."

"Why had our office not been informed via the Fusion Center?" Suzanne Sanchez inquired.

"Your office is now informed via you, Ms. Sanchez," Bersconi said curtly. "The objective is fusion, not confusion."

"You said biological weapons. Can you explain?" Sean said.

"That's the sketchiest part. No is the best answer. We don't believe conventional weapons are involved. Only human bodies. Nature of the attack unknown," the Special Agent replied.

"So we are preparing for an attack somewhere, sometime, somehow by unarmed enslaved Haitians, brainwashed or otherwise motivated?" said Sanchez, her sarcastic tone building. "Excuse me if I seem insensitive or politically incorrect, but it sounds like you're asking us to prepare for an attack of the zombies."

After a long uncomfortable silence Sean inquired diplomatically, "Are there any specific actions you are recommending?"

"Paul?" Bersconi said, looking at Stearns.

"State Department is deferring to the FBI for the time being," he answered.

"We recommend no action at this time. We brought you here to stay a step ahead of whatever is coming. Keep the information confidential and need to know. I'll be in touch," said Bernaconi signaling the meetings conclusion.

Sean wondered if it was the royal we, or the controlling I, that rankled him. He noted that Sanchez appreciated neither.

CHAPTER 25

"Changes in states of consciousness," Professor Melissa White told the Harvard class, "change the physical structure of the brain. The brain is the organ that reveals the mind, but it is the mind that shapes the brain. Some would have you believe it is the other way around."

"Professor?" Ketia raised her hand with a question.

White knew that Ketia didn't need to take her popular undergraduate class to fulfill a requirement. She audited the class with her approval purely from interest. In an age of credential seekers White found that refreshing. She'd recently hired her into a part-time nurse position at the Institute while she worked on her Public Health graduate degree.

"Yes Ketia."

"Would this also be true when a subject is unconscious. Sleeping. Dreaming say. Could dreams shape the brain?"

"Most certainly. Despite research by the eminent Professor Hobson and others implying that rapid eye movement causes dreams. And despite the preposterous claims by decades of researchers that the source of all human mentation must be organic. The very nature of dreams completely refutes this."

"How so?"

"Recall the lecture on Dreams and Indigenous Societies. Until medieval times even the western world concurred with all societies that dreaming helped shape human activity. What was then called the visium is now called lucid dreaming. Contemporary science has chosen to ignore this realm partly because no research instrument can detect this state. Yet we know it exists because we all experience lucid dreams. We know we are asleep…

unconscious by definition ... but we are aware that we are dreaming. Our minds are capable of directing these dreams."

White paused and took in the confused expressions of Ketia and her classmates.

"There is no evidence of any physical origin for these dreams. Some would have you believe they are simple manifestations of agitations from the brain stem. But they are not simple. They are bizarrely complex. And what agitates the brain stem? Who? You do. Your mind."

White could see that the class still had not been entirely convinced. She acknowledged the raised hand of the pale, curly haired young man whom she considered congenitally disputatious.

"Professor. A person blind from birth has no visual realm, therefore no visium. What sort of lucid dream could such a person possibly direct?"

"Harold you are being semantic. Those blind from birth report no visual realm to their dreams. But they do dream in the same way they live. And they have lucid dreams. Dreams of flying and landing in places where they can feel the grass against their feet."

Harold appeared unconvinced but remained silent.

"As you all know, one of the challenges of this class is to demonstrate a thread…a string if you will…connecting history and dreams. So, here is the assignment for next week. I want you all to bring in one historical example of a future event evidenced in the past. Believe me there are many to be found. I'll give you a good example. In Morgan Robertson's 1898 novella *Futility* a British ship called the Titan hits an iceberg starboard near midnight in April sinking to the bottom of the North Atlantic on its maiden voyage. Each of these details is also true of the Titanic's demise in 1912. Both ships were eight-hundred feet long, made of steel with three props, two masts and a carrying capacity of three-thousand passengers. Deemed unsinkable they carried an insufficient number of lifeboats. There are additional striking similarities, but the biggest difference is that one ship is real while the other is not."

White paused for effect.

"At least that is what history tells us."

Ketia put down her glass and Sean immediately replenished it from a bottle of Chianti they shared. They sat at an open window table at the front of the Caffé Pompei on Hanover Street enjoying the evening. Sean's apartment was right around the corner and this table was one of his favorite people watching spots.

"So what do think? Nice huh?" Sean prompted.

"It's a great spot. I've hardly ever been to the North End. Another side of the world from Dorchester."

"I grew up in Dorchester. Neponset."

"Another side of the world from Codman Square. Dorchester. Where I grew up."

"Really? My father grew up there. He has some stories."

"I'd like to hear them sometime."

"No you wouldn't."

"Well then tell me about you. Your work."

"Ladies first."

"Well I recently joined the Talbot Institute as a part-time nurse. I just got my business cards. You're the first person I gave one to. I look after twelve, well eleven since one died this week, mostly wealthy resident patients. And you know about the Health Center. I do whatever they need. Runs the gamut. I'm there about ten hours per week. Unpaid but I get internship credit toward my degree in Public Health."

"Rich, poor and everyone in between. Full service provider. Oh. Sorry. I have to take this," said Sean retrieving his phone from a pocket.

Sean stepped away and around the corner to take his call. When he returned a minute later Ketia could read his face.

"Let me guess. Emergency. You have to go."

"I'm sorry. Heck of a first date, huh?"

"And I never even found out what you do, Mister Deputy Chief of the Boston Police Department Regional Intelligence Center."

"This is it. Basically."

*

Instead of sitting at a café table in the North End with an enchanting date, Sean got to sit in a sterile conference room at FBI headquarters with Special Agent Bersconi and Paul Stearns from the State Department. Taking his date away was one thing, replacing her with these ugly mugs was uncivilized.

"Aren't we going to wait for Ms. Sanchez from Homeland?" Sean said as Bersconi was just getting started.

"This is need to know. We need specific action by the city within a limited locale. If that need expands we'll bring her in."

"How can I help?"

"We've lost contact with our agent in the Dorchester Haitian community. You have a lot of eyes and ears we can enlist to help find him. But…"

"But we can't tell our police officers who they are looking for or why without compromising the operation."

"Exactly."

"Again. How can I help?"

"Paul why don't you go ahead," Bersconi said.

"Sure. Sean, we'd like your officers to step up surveillance in the arenas where illegal immigrant labor typically manifests itself. Sweat shops, scrub kitchens, massage parlors, domestic and motel housekeeping. Look for anything unusual, spikes in activity, shifts or concentrations. Bizarre behavior."

"Bizarre behavior?"

"Take a look into the vodoun community," Bersconi said.

"And?"

"See anything strange let us know."

CHAPTER 26

Of the six patients in the experimental wing at Talbot Sam Stockton was the star contributor to research efforts. Stockton was autistic and severely narcoleptic.

All the patients except Stockton spent much of their sleeping time hooked to computer programs that monitored and interpreted dream imagery. Technology recently invented at UC Berkeley allowed computers to generate words from brain waves. White and Meacham had some limited success adapting the UC program to provide transcripts of dialogue from within a dream. Sam Stockton was also wired to a new program they developed that reversed the process by "playing" encoded images and scripts provided by White. Meacham developed and added auditory cues and olfactory stimuli. Essentially a screenplay was looped through Stockton's brain in sleep state. Part power of suggestion, part biochemical stimulus, the experiment was beginning to show promising results.

Meacham and White stood over a sleeping Sam Stockton studying the scan imagery and data on their equipment.

"I knew you'd be pleased. What I don't understand is why you seem to be placing undue significance on the content of his report. Fact is that he reported as influenced. That is substantial. Why embellish?" Meacham said.

"Because he did embellish. Not only that but he validated the script verbally. Look. My students devised all the previous narratives. Simple plots. Sunny day at the beach. Walk in the woods."

"You're oversimplifying."

"Alright, but you get the point. One day I'm getting coffee at the Dunkin Donuts down at the corner and I decided to walk across the street and finally read that historic marker that I've ignored for years."

"Moswetuset Hummock."

"Right. I didn't know you cared about history. So you know then. The Institute sits here on the end of an Indian trail that goes through Dorchester up the hill along Centre Street to Codman Square and along Norfolk Street to the Blue Hills."

"So what?"

"So the history intrigued me and I did a bit of research. I thought hey, this stuff would make a great dream narrative. So I wrote it up for Sam."

"And?"

"The point is my students didn't write the content this time. I did. I know every detail and nuance in the program. There was no mention of a Liberty Tree Tavern. Sam embellished. So I did some more research. There was an actual Liberty Tree Tavern in 1775 on the Upper Road, now Washington Street in Codman Square. He pulled that in. I can show you the exact peak on the REM charts. It doesn't correlate to the programming. It is a tangent. A string."

Meacham fixed his eyes on Melissa White for a long silent moment.

"Nonsense," he said.

He turned and walked away.

CHAPTER 27

As he walked into the District C-11 Fields Corner Police Station Sean thought that he should have assigned the lead on the FBI request to staff. He had enough on his plate and didn't need voodoo as dessert. But given the sensitivity he figured the fewer involved the better.

He was on good terms with the Captain so it presented no problem skipping down the chain of command to his high school buddy, Tim Mooney, directly with the request. Keeping it all on a need to know basis. Tim was a Lieutenant. He was diligent and trustworthy. Most importantly he was discrete.

"Good to see you Sean old buddy," said Lieutenant Mooney with a strong handshake. "Let me introduce you. Sean Leahy, this is Sergeant Anthony Sebastiene and Detective Andrea Coles. They of course know of you, and are pleased to be of assistance. They are both lifelong Dorchester residents of Haitian heritage and probably the best eyes and ears we can provide you within the community."

Sean greeted both the officers noting that the Sergeant was his father's age and the Detective was considerably younger.

"I grew up in Neponset," Sean said. "How about you?" he said, his eyes going first to Detective Coles then to Sergeant Sebastiene.

"Right here in Fields Corner all my life," said Coles.

"Codman Square all mine," said Sebastiene.

"My father grew up there," Sean said to the Sergeant.

Tony focused on the name Leahy, picturing Finn in his mind. He noted the resemblance. But he said nothing.

Sean zeroed in on Tony's consternation. "You have a concern Sergeant?"

"No. Not at all. I was just… I had a boyhood friend… a resemblance… his name was Finn Leahy."

"That would be my father."

*

As requested Sergeant Sebastiene and Detective Coles briefed Sean on current activity within highly secretive Vodoun circles. They knew of a recent meeting of oungan and manbos, priests and priestesses. They heard whisperings about possessed spirits walking the streets and of the need for cleansing rituals. Sean asked about location. He was told that the general vicinity of Codman Square appeared to be the epicenter. He asked them to try to refine the location and report back in three days.

After the briefing Sergeant Sebastiene approached him and asked about Finn. Sean said he was sure his father would no doubt be thrilled to reconnect with his boyhood pal. He promised to put him in touch. Sean left the District police office and started toward Fields Corner T station but changed his mind and did an about face on Gibson Street. It was less than ten blocks to his father's apartment on Adams Street. Finn should be getting home from the garage right about now. Sean called him. Finn said he was just stepping into the shower but he'd be glad to have him come by for a beer. Sean checked his voice mail and returned a few calls as he walked. He rang the bell at the apartment and Finn buzzed him right in.

"Called you at the garage yesterday and Lenny said you called in sick. You didn't pick up when I called here, but I did get your message that you were ok. What's up? You never call in sick."

"Had a mind-splitting headache. I'm fine today," Finn lied.

"You sure Pops? You don't look so great."

Finn almost told Sean about the box. But the part of him that wanted to cry out for help remained silent. "Maybe I got a little flu or somethin'. I'm gonna have a cup of tea. Wants some? Or a beer?"

"Tea, huh? Now I know you're not right. Sure, I'll have some tea."

"What brings you around Dorchester?"

"Had a meeting at the police station. Met a Sergeant named Sebastiene. Says you two are old buds. He'd like to reconnect."

"Tony. No shit. Yeah, we had some times. Haven't seen him since we were teenagers. Cop, huh? That figures. He was always the good kid. You thought your mother rode you? You shoulda seen his old lady in action."

"I guess without women like them the bad guys would have us outnumbered. Here. He gave me his card for you."

"Thanks. I'll call him."

CHAPTER 28

"Professor may I speak frankly?" Harold said from his usual seat in the front row of the lecture hall.

"By all means, Harold. Go right ahead. You couldn't speak otherwise. But honestly. I find it refreshing," Professor White replied.

"Today's *Harvard Crimson* called this class a joke, and compared your string theory approach with Timothy Leary's LSD classes in the sixties. Here's my question. Would it be possible to get an A on the final if a student were to employ a strategy of using the exam to refute all that you are proposing?"

"Absolutely. As long as the student remained within the context of the question, utilized the material presented, and adhered to the literature. Yes. Such a strategy would have the same chance for a grade of A as a student employing a different one, say…well, a constructive strategy for example."

While White emphasized the word *constructive* she picked up a copy of the *Crimson* and held it before the class.

"The reporter did a factual job, but missed certain opportunities and nuances in her story. Professor Leary began by investigating a frontier of the mind, as are we. Such endeavors should always be acknowledged as admirable, but he moved beyond the academic fringe and thus failed. We have not. He studied the illusory unchartered psychedelic realm. We study the scientific literature of dreams. He grounded his work in hallucinogenic drugs. We ground ours in contemporary physics."

White removed the page containing the referenced story from the body of the newspaper and constructed a paper airplane as she spoke.

"The most noted omission here is Leary's mantra. 'Turn on. Tune in. Drop out.' I should like to have seen that juxtaposed in the article against quotations representive of our quest. Martin Luther King's 'I have a dream.' Shakespeare's 'Such stuff as dreams are made on.' And perhaps a reference to the timeless sage advisement to 'Follow your dreams'."

White sailed the paper airplane into a nearby trashcan.

"How about 'Row, row, row your boat'?" Harold said.

Melissa White thanked Chris Sebastiene for coming, and escorted him to the Institute's front door before returning to her desk. She was quite impressed with the young man. She'd showed him the server room and discussed the programming objectives. Chris was both a software and a hardware guru. Tough to find. Like a student who cares about the subject matter as much as the grade or credential.

He'd be a good complement to Ketia on their team. As soon as she cleared the finances with Meacham she intended to make an offer and bring Chris on board at Talbot. Her desk phone rang and she picked up.

"Talbot Institute. Melissa White speaking."

"Hello Doctor White. Or is it Professor White?"

"Either is correct. With whom am I speaking?"

This is Matthew Dougherty, Boston Herald. Have time for a few questions?"

"I don't know why I should. That was a horribly misleading piece you ran last week."

"Nothing but the facts, Doctor. Pure journalism."

"Facts wrapped in innuendo and spun with undue suspicion."

"I assume you read the story on your class in the *Harvard Crimson* yesterday. Any comment?"

"Same observation I shared with my class. Endeavors on the frontiers of the mind should always be acknowledged as admirable."

"Are you and Doctor Meacham doing admirable work there at Talbot?"

"I already described our work to you. Doctor Meacham and I use some of the same data but our projects are independent. Michael's work is in neurophysiology and psychopharmacology. My work is in psychology, specifically dream study. And yes, my work is admirable."

"And Doctor Meacham's?"

"You're asking if his work is admirable? It seems so to me. You should ask him."

"Do you have many Haitians at Talbot?"

"Excuse me? What kind of a question is that?"

"Straight forward. Do you have many Haitians at Talbot?"

"As far as staff goes, we are an equal opportunity employer. As for patients, that information is client-patient confidential."

"Are you doing quantum research at Talbot?"

"See? There you go. That's a misleading question. The undergraduate class I teach at Harvard…the one in the *Crimson* story… is not affiliated with the experimental work here at Talbot."

"One more question. Does your work involve the practice of Voodoo?"

"Totally ridiculous!"

"Does it?"

"Of course not."

"Thanks Doc. Have a nice day."

CHAPTER 29

The second night Tony and Detective Andrea Coles sniffed around Vodoun haunts they heard a commotion on Southern Avenue. Coles was undercover as a streetwalker. She alerted him on her wire. Tony stayed cautiously nearby in his unmarked car. Since most people in the neighborhood knew his face, he was relegated to the back up role. He hated the lonely assignment.

A small mob congregated near the old Synagogue by the New England Avenue tracks. From his vantage point Tony could see an individual moving wildly in the middle of a circle of containment. The youth, or at least Tony assumed he was because his head was concealed by a sweatshirt hood, broke free. He charged up the stairs of a three decker and into the foyer. The crowd grew quiet. Two shotgun blasts vibrated the night air like a sonic boom. The crowd scattered. Tony jumped out of the car and ran toward Coles, weapon drawn.

He and Coles moved cautiously into the foyer of the house. The hooded individual lay at the threshold, mostly sans torso.

Coles held her weapon pointed at the thin, balding white guy in a tank-top tee shirt emphasizing his excessive arm-pit hair.

"My house. I'm standing my ground," the guy said. Then he placed the shotgun onto the floor.

*

"Meacham speaking."

"Good afternoon Doctor. This is Matthew Dougherty with the Herald. How are you today?"

"I was doing fine."

"Ha. Just take a minute of your time. I'm following up on the dream research story at Talbot."

"Why talk to me? You'll write whatever you want anyway."

"Is your work at Talbot admirable?"

"Is yours?"

"Of course."

"Then we have something in common after all. Look ah, Dougherty, if you stick to the research details I'll give you a minute."

"Fair enough. What type of drugs do you use on the subjects?"

"There is no drug administration per se. A mild hypnotic occasionally. We work within the subjects given cognitive orientations."

"Ever bring your research into the Haitian community?"

"Why would I do that?"

"That was my next question."

"I don't know what you're talking about. Sorry I am out of time. Good day."

*

The bus stop on Talbot Avenue with the bench was her favorite. Rarely did she get on the bus. She usually moved back to another stop just before one arrived. Few people ever noticed her. Those who did saw only a bag lady. They did not see her. For the rare encounter she carried church literature. The pamphlets were amazingly effective repellants.

Her heightened senses brought her a world unknown to most. She observed. This was her craft and she was expert. The unpleasant smell of decay she noticed at this bench earlier was stronger. She followed it to a house a considerable distance down Southern Avenue.

She went into the foyer where there were three mailboxes. The first floor door was open. She could see a middle-aged white man with wavy gray hair sitting at the kitchen table. He was staring at a photo of a young couple captured at the beach. She called out to him but he did not acknowledge her. She left a pamphlet in the mailbox and climbed to the second flat. The door was open. The stench was unbearable. Stepping inside she saw the source. The body of a very thin white man in a tank-top shirt was sprawled on the living room floor. She thought he was dead but then his eyes twinkled at her. It took her a moment to process what she was seeing. Yes, he was dead. The twinkles were flies feasting on his open eyes. There were ceremonial cuts on his flesh. He lay in a circle of personal items. His head was oddly askance as if his neck was broken.

Her sense was that much of this was a fleeting apparition. She went back down the stairs and left pamphlets in the remaining two mailboxes. On her way back to the bus stop she went to three more houses distributing pamphlets. Then she stopped at a pay phone, dialed 911 and reported the death anonymously. She did not expect them to find exactly what she had seen.

*

Lt. Mooney closed the door to his office after Sergeant Sebastiene and Detective Coles sat down.

"The guy who 'stood his ground' with the shotgun last night on the home invasion was an FBI agent, so you did the right thing by not arresting him."

"What's he doing living on Southern Avenue?" Coles said.

"What's he doing blowing away teenagers?" Tony said.

"Don't know. I'd have you bring him in and ask him except he's dead."

"Lieutenant?" Tony said.

"Morning shift responded to an anonymous call. Found him on the second floor flat with his neck broken and cut up pretty bad. I called Sean Leahy about last night's shooting. He got in touch with the FBI, since it fit their "suspicious" criteria, and they told him the victim was one of their agents. One of two they have under deep cover in Codman Square. Had under deep cover. The other one is missing."

"What's going on Lieutenant?" Coles said.

"All we know is that they think there's a Haitian terrorist cell plotting an attack with a biological weapon. They're being pretty damned closed mouth on us. Just key on illegal immigrants and voodoo they say."

"That's all we got?" Tony said.

"Not much, I know. More than you knew yesterday. Keep it confidential. That's all we have. Be safe."

CHAPTER 30

Tony enjoyed reuniting with Finn over lunch and then for after work beers at the Blarney Stone in Fields Corner. The decades in between seemed but weeks. They made each other feel young at heart. But Tony sensed there was something bothering Finn below the surface. And when Finn called him again yesterday he sounded troubled.

Tony said the Eire Pub would be a fine place to meet. He parked his car at the curb in front just as Finn approached on foot from his nearby apartment.

"Hey there Finn old man. How ya doin'?"

"Not such a bad day. Yourself?"

"Be better after you buy me a beer."

"Hey it's happy hour right? Let's go in and I'll do just that."

"Actually it's two thirty. And happy hour has been illegal in Boston for what, twenty years now?"

"Its beer thirty somewhere. And I'm finished at the shop."

"My day off and you're buyin'. Perfect."

Finn smacked Tony on the back a few times and held the door as they entered. A few heads turned and Tony returned the glances. Finn noticed.

"This place is alright," he said. "Black guys been comin' in here since we was kids…almost."

"Ain't the color of my skin. It's because I'm a cop. Most likely they don't know that but they sense it. Something about movement. We learn to walk the street differently. Enter a room cautiously. Becomes second nature after awhile. People see it. Even if they don't know what they're seein'."

They settled into their stools and ordered a couple of drafts.

"Get the fresh catch swordfish if you're hungry," Finn said. "Best piece of fish in Boston."

"I heard the roast beef sandwich is the way to go."

"Used to be, maybe still, but if you want a sandwich go for the corned beef."

"Some of us are trying to lay off the grease."

"Some of us?"

"You heard right."

Finn smiled.

"I've been here a few times," Tony said. "Good place. Never been here on a call. No trouble here."

"Not like places in the Square, huh?" said Finn.

"There ain't many bars there nowadays. Not like when we were kids. The few that are open today can be trouble. But if you recall, all the bars were trouble back then."

"Norfolk Tavern for sure. So they don't need bars now cause they're all doin' dope?"

"They? They is a lot of different folks. Yeah, there's dope. But mostly the cultures changed. The Irish took their bars with them."

"Fair enough. Maybe we should give a few back. Might mellow out all the violence."

"Codman Square has always been violent. Hell Finn, we were violent."

"I know. It's just that we had the opportunity to change. And we did. The place nowadays is over the top."

"No, it's just different than it was. Different people. Same struggles."

"C'mon Tony. We ruled those streets. Now I'm afraid to walk them."

"I still walk."

"Right. And you still rule. With a badge and a semi-automatic."

"I mean off duty. I raised my family there. I have grandkids. It's not like you think."

"Fuck it isn't. Thirteen year old gangsters poppin' each other for a cell phone."

"You stole cars. Mike got shot. Remember?"

"I remember. It's rampant today. The violence is epidemic Tony."

"It was for awhile. Especially in the 70's while the cultures were shifting. But we got a handle on it. Things are much better today."

"Not from outside looking in. Not from the stats you keep at your station house."

"Well if we're talking specifically about black male on black male teen violence…"

"Specifically exactly."

"…then you're right. But that problem isn't just Codman Square, or Boston, or any black neighborhood in any city for that matter. It's an American problem. It's your problem and my problem. And you don't fix problems by moving away from them."

"Good luck Tony. That's all I can say. And hang onto your gun when you retire."

"No. Look at it this way. You like cars. When we were kids people could drive them around with a bottle of booze between their legs and toss the bottle out the window when it was empty. There were no laws against any of that. But then driving became epidemic. All kinds of laws were enacted. We got a whole book now. Vehicle Code. Seat belt laws, blood alcohol levels, cell phone use."

"So you tellin' me we need a code book for black kids?"

"No. I'm telling you that we addressed the problems created by rampant vehicle use over the years as we realized the dangers."

"Kids in my neighborhood aren't driving around shooting each other."

"You don't get it. Listen. That's where the analogy ends. First of all, inner city kids mostly don't have cars. And even if they did, there wouldn't be all those Mothers Against Drunk Driving groups lookin' after their well-being. That's the point. They have no advocates. We recognized the dangers of vehicle use and took action over time. Still do. We long ago recognized the dangers these inner city kids present to themselves and did nothing. And we still don't."

Tony used Finn's uncharacteristic silence as momentum.

"You said you wanted to meet and tell me something about old times in Codman Square. I got an idea. C'mon. Let's go." He said standing.

"What? Where?" Finn said without realizing he also had stood.

"Time you had a real look at your old neighborhood," Tony said as he gently directed Finn toward the door.

A few heads turned and Tony returned the glances. After they left someone asked if Finn had just been arrested.

*

Ketia went through her routine at Talbot efficiently. She always went through the six rooms of the experimental wing first. She recorded the blood pressure and pulse of each patient. Made sure any drip lines remained secure. Administered meds. Changed bedpans. Prodded torsos. Fluffed pillows. She spoke to each of them kindly, however unresponsive. Only Sam Stockton ever spoke. He never looked at her. And whatever he said hardly ever seemed appropriate to time and place. If it did Ketia assumed it coincidental. This morning he had said, "Watch out for that bastard."

Ketia was surprised to see a woman in Arthur Ludlow's bed as she moved onto the residential wing. Then she remembered that a new patient was to be admitted. She looked at Ms. Winston's chart. Comatose. Brain tumor. Terminal. Do not resuscitate. She felt for her pulse on the left wrist.

Ketia leaped away as she felt the push back. The patient sat bolt upright staring ahead with eyes wide open, right arm extended with index finger pointing. Despite all the motion the patient did not appear conscious to Ketia. But then she spoke.

"There he is!" she screeched venomously. Then she collapsed back to the position in which Ketia had found her. Eyes closed.

Ketia took a deep breath. She reached for a pulse and was startled again. Only this time it was by a sudden voice. Too loud. Too close.

"What is going on in here?" Doctor Meacham demanded as he came further into the room.

*

They sat at the small bar inside the Ashmont Grille. Tony got to drive only as far as the Ashmont T Station when Finn insisted on getting out and taking the Mattapan Trolley to the Cedar Grove stop and home. Tony was able to park and dissuade Finn with the offer of another beer and a ride home.

"Remember how we used to walk by this place then catch the trolley to Mattapan for a double feature matinee at the Oriental Theater on summer days?" Tony said.

"Yeah, and there'd be guys stumbling in and out the door here by noon, and you could almost get drunk on the fumes that wafted onto the sidewalk."

"Well look at it now. Place has class. Good menu. Atmosphere."

"What are you trying to tell me."

"Place got a second life. It resonates hope for the neighborhood."

"This ain't Codman Square. This is Peabody Square."

"They butt into each other for cryin out loud. This is the edge. The cutting edge."

"Everyplace got an edge." Finn picked up a menu and studied it for a moment. "They servin' soba noodles and wasabi up the hill?"

"No but there's good island food and yes some Asian. You'd be surprised. Let's walk. Like we did when we were kids. Tell me what you got on your mind. Turn back whenever you say."

"I think I liked this place better before it got reborn. Back when it stank before it died," said Finn as he shrugged, reluctantly indicating he would go along.

CHAPTER 31

As they walked up Talbot Avenue from Peabody Square, Finn and Tony talked about old times a bit before Tony pressed.

"You have something to say, mind telling me what?"

"Yeah, yeah right. Well, I got all this junk from the past, you know. Sometimes I look through it, mostly I don't. Maybe ten, fifteen years since I looked through some of it. Sean's little league days, wedding pictures. Most of it makes me feel good, some bad."

"Same as everybody."

"I looked through some stuff from when we were kids. Remember when I got that box from the Codman tomb?"

"Shit yeah. Don't see stuff like that happen everyday."

"I still have it. Looked at it the other day. Been having nightmares ever since."

"If I went into that tomb, I'd a never stopped having nightmares."

"Thing is that it's always the same nightmare. I had it for a while when I first got the box. It came back every time I touched the thing so I put it away for years and forgot about it. Took it out maybe ten years ago, nightmare came back."

"So toss it. No more box. No more reminder. No more nightmare."

"Maybe. But I got this feeling that would be bad for me. You see I don't just dream. I walk. I wake up in another room standing in a cold sweat. Someone's yelling at me to step back. There is this ledge and a bright light. Sounds crazy but I think if I don't step back, if I don't walk in my sleep and wake up, I'll die. I think I'm supposed to deliver this box. Can you help me?"

"I'm a cop not a shrink, Finn. Maybe you should talk to someone about it. Some of the guys I work with get bad dreams. Trouble sleeping. Stress. We get them into counseling. Seems to help more often than not."

"Nah. Ruth and I saw a counselor when we were splitting up. A woman. She was on Ruth's side. So we switched to a man. He was on her side too. I said you can't help me buddy. He said I can't help you if you won't help yourself. I said if I can help myself why am I paying you. Waste of time."

They had walked all the way to Codman Square to the intersection of Talbot and Norfolk. Tony paused. "As I remember, the crate containing the box was stolen from, and recovered by, the Museum of Fine Arts. Let me speak with the security chief over there, nose around a bit," he said.

"Graveyard's right down there," Finn said, pointing down Norfolk Street. "Maybe I should just go put it back."

"Something 'bout two wrongs don't make a right at play there I think. But we might walk that way so you can see how little the landscape has changed. You know this was an Indian trail. I suspect that whole graveyard was always an open field, least since the natives opened it with fire. Probably set up a seasonal camp there. Hell, old Codman might of had his bones entombed right on top of a sacred site."

As they walked down Norfolk Tony glanced at Finn and saw that he was visibly shaken.

"On second thought I'll show you what's become of Kaspar's Market," he said as he turned Finn right and steered them down Whitfield Street instead.

At sunset Dr. Michael Meacham walked from his MGH office into the maze of locks that regulated the flow of the Charles River, allowing boat traffic down to the ocean and pedestrian passage across to Charlestown. About midway he stopped and contemplated the water. After a few minutes a bearded man in a rasta cap and sunglasses approached the railing. The little of his face that was exposed revealed a dark complexion bordered in dreads. Meacham removed something from his pocket and slid it across the railing enclosed in his hand. The man took it and slid something back. When the exchange was completed the rasta man walked off toward Charlestown. Meacham waited a minute and then began walking back toward the hospital. From a nearby lock Dougherty abruptly turned and walked away unnoticed. The Herald reporter knew Meacham was dirty but he still needed to find out why.

*

The short one-way stretch of Whitfield Street connecting Norfolk with Southern Avenue consisted mostly of three decker houses occupied by African-American families. At certain times of the day there was considerable foot traffic as it provided a short cut to some areas of the Square. As they walked toward the old Kaspar Brothers Market Tony and Finn saw no one except the obscured silhouette of a person behind the wheel of a sedan parked in the traffic lane.

"That's what I'm talking about," Finn said. "That joker's parked in the middle of the street facing against the traffic. Place is uncivilized."

Before Tony could respond, a blur of a male figure raced down the steps of a house and jumped into the sedan. The driver peeled out, and away toward Southern Avenue, side swiping a parked vehicle enroute.

"Whoa," said Tony, the cop in him making a mental note of the make and model.

"White four-door 2003 Pontiac Vibe," Finn called out with a mechanic's precision that he knew would test Tony's observational skill. "Two asshole occupants."

"Slow up a bit Finn while I call this in."

They came to a stop by the steps where the man ran down. Tony noted the address and speed dialed his dispatcher.

"Watch out," yelled Finn, shoving Tony, who was involved in his cell phone call. A middle-aged black man stumbled down the steps and right through the space where Tony had been standing.

"What the fuck you doin' pal?" said Finn. The man paid no attention as he continued stumbling slowly into the street.

Tony stashed his phone, grabbed the man by the shoulders and spun him around. The guy continued to stumble in place going nowhere as Tony held him.

"Jezzuz," said Finn, "he doesn't even look conscious."

"Give me a hand." Tony felt the man becoming a dead weight so he eased him to the pavement with Finn's help.

Finn stepped away while Tony did a quick medical assessment.

"Want me to dial 911?" Finn said as he pulled out his cell phone.

"Get an ambulance," said Tony as he started chest compressions. "But it ain't gonna help. He's dead."

CHAPTER 32

Having taught this class for several semesters Mellisa White knew her lecture on quantum physics was the most difficult and critical material for her dream psychology students. She liked to think her delivery improved each semester. She thought today's lecture had gone well so far.

"Quantum physicists have a problem that classic physicists do not share. In quantum reality a particle travels more than one route to arrive at a specific destination. Classic physics, and human logic, say no way. One particle. One way. One destination please. When a physicist observes the movement of a particle then only this classic result is achieved. One route. Such are the limitations of human perception.

An unobserved particle travels according to quantum model mathematical predictions. Multiple routes. But it seems that by observing the experiment the results are inadvertently altered. We cause it to be only where we can see."

White looked out at a sea of blank faces.

"The easiest way to comprehend this paradox is to accept that everything has both a particle feature and a wave feature. These features are complementary."

Ketia and a few others nodded. Lights were coming on.

"Thinking that something will travel conventionally because it has substance is an incomplete prediction because it does not include the wave feature. Thinking that something will travel multiple routes simultaneously because it is a wave is an incomplete prediction because it does not include the substance feature. A complete picture of physical reality requires that both features be taken into account."

"What does this have to do with dreams?" Harold said.

"Ah ha! Thank you Harold. We have a similar problem with dreams. Classic researchers tell us that dreams are simply the sleeping brain reacting to brain stem agitations. And they overlook the fact that by observing our dream we can alter it. No question there is an organic feature to dreaming. The particle. The substance. But there is also a conscious feature involved. The wave. The mind. You. A complete picture of dream reality requires that both features be taken into account."

White looked away from Harold.

"Now I would like to defer questions and use the remaining time for discussion. Comment anyone? Politely please. One at a time."

"If everything has a wave feature then that must mean our bodies, our molecular structure has this feature. I'm thinking that maybe dreams are possibly the most observable wavelike feature. I mean look at the equipment researchers use. The dream data mostly shows as waves," observed a student in the back of the lecture hall.

"Surfing dreams are cool," Harold said.

"I like the notion of the observer altering the observation. If the dream is not observed did it happen? Why? Kind of like the tree falling in the woods," commented Ketia.

"Seems to me that classic researchers have wasted years of lab time only to conclude that dreams are nothing more than the brain hopelessly trying to make sense of jittery nerves. I hope we can find something grander. I think the history of humankind requires that we do," said another student.

Professor White let them go on for the remaining minutes of class. When all the students had departed she walked out of the room thoroughly pleased.

CHAPTER 33

Meacham walked out of the locks and hailed a cab in front of the TD Garden. Dougherty managed to follow in his car. They drove to Inman Square in

Cambridge. Meacham deliberately exited the cab short of his destination and walked down a few dimly-lighted side streets to a two-family house. Dougherty parked hastily at a hydrant. He was about to lose sight of Meacham when he saw him enter a house. He pulled out and drove past, noting the address. Then he parked again and waited.

Meacham climbed the interior staircase to the upper flat where he knocked three times on the door. The door opened as far as the chain allowed. A bespectacled man with a Nordic face and cautious eyes peered out.

"Meacham. You should have called."

"Since when do I call? Are you doing take out now Nils? Open please."

Before relocating to Cambridge Nils Osterman obtained a PhD in organic chemistry at Clemson University. His dissertation involved the development of a substance known as JWH-018 that later found its way around the globe in an underground synthetic marijuana product called Spice. In Cambridge Osterman altered the product and repackaged it under several names. He sold the product legally on-line to head shop distributors using an overseas account. This avocation aside, Osterman was a brilliant chemist known throughout academia and industry. He was under contract by Meacham for the research at Talbot Institute.

Nils unlocked the door and Meacham entered. They headed to the large kitchen table where they customarily did business.

"This is…is my friend Thomas."

Meacham was surprised to see someone at the table. Nils was a loner. Meacham had never seen anyone at the flat before.

"Hello. I'm Michael," Meacham said, purposely keeping it to a first name basis.

"Pleased to meet you Michael. I was just leaving. Take care. See you Nils."

The slender young black man stood and walked out. Meacham noticed he carried an aluminum medical case with him. The kind used to transport blood samples or body parts.

"Who's he?" Meacham said after he heard the door shut.

"Just a neighbor," said Nils.

Meacham thought Nils was lying but let it go.

"Here smell this," Nils said, pushing a small pot in front of Meacham and pouring boiling water into it.

Meacham sniffed the steam pensively.

"Get it?"

"Almost," Meacham said and sniffed again. "Smells like the subway."

"Correct. Now this," said Nils as he poured water into another pot.

"That is completely disgusting," said Meacham pushing it aside after a brief sniff.

"Guess?"

"Don't care to."

"Franklin Park Zoo Gorilla enclosure," Nils said, looking rather pleased.

"Why would you make these smells? Who'd want them?" Meacham said incredulously.

"Just the challenge. And you never know how they might come in handy. When your Institute paid me to fabricate the smell of an historic tavern, I already had the soppy floor of New York's McSorley's Old Ale House in my cabinet."

"But a monkey house? Never mind. Have you received the shipment yet? I am running low."

"I received the ayahuasca today. The zolipidem should arrive tomorrow. If not I'll extract the base from some Ambien or Edular."

"Fine. I'll come back tomorrow."

"Meacham I want you to know that obtaining ayahuasca legally is increasingly arduous. You may want to investigate alternative avenues of procurement."

Meacham poured two lines of cocaine from the bindle he bought from the rasta man. He snorted a long line and slid the mirror over to Nils.

"Wonderful," Meacham said sarcastically. "And here I was hoping that you'd find a way to procure this stuff here for me legally."

*

The paramedics did their obligatory drill and passed the body off to the coroner. While the detectives wrapped up loose ends with the neighbors, Finn and Tony walked the short distance down to the old Kaspar Brothers Market and waited outside. Soon one of the detectives would join them where they could all talk away from neighbors' ears.

"How many times we run around this place as kids? You, me, Mike. Hundreds? Thousands?" Tony said.

"Damn strange piece of architecture isn't it? One-story, streets on three sides, no window except at the front, like a little fortress," Finn said.

"What were there like five, six brothers? I remember one of the older ones would sell us beer for a two-dollar mark up when we were only fifteen."

"There was the nice one who gave us free Cokes and Hostess cupcakes when we were younger. But the hired guy who loaded the delivery truck at the back door was the best."

"I forget."

"You weren't quite ready for his stories at the time as I recall," Finn said. "We all thought he was the coolest, most knowledgeable dude in the world. I guess he might have been all of twenty-one or two. He'd tell us in fine detail about girls whose pants he'd gotten into. Always a new one, new details. Don't know how many times I went to confession about the dirty thoughts I had at night about that. That's what we called them, dirty thoughts. Priest would always ask if there was anything else. Bastard knew, but I never told him. Of course then I'd feel bad about not having a full confession, and the guilt would just build."

"Glad I wasn't a practicing Catholic," Tony said.

"Now the new Haitians coming in got it all mixed up with magic. Your old priest wouldn't know what to make of it."

"Hey Sarge, sorry for the wait," the detective said as he approached.

"How did it go back at the house, Ken?" Tony said.

"First two floors completely empty. Dead guy had no ID. People on the third say they know nothing about him or anything going on. Same with the neighbors on either side. They all seemed scared and like they was holding something back."

Tony introduced Finn and stepped aside while he filled the detective in on what they had seen. After Tony corroborated, the detective asked him if the dead guy seemed drunk.

"Not drunk. More like a seizure, but not quite…"

"He was like a zombie," Finn said.

"Yeah that's it, like in a bad movie," Tony said. "But that's not the weirdest part. When I spun the guy around and looked at him. He looked like he was already dead. While he was still standing."

"That's funny," the detective said.

"How so?"

"The coroner asked the medics how long the guy had been down. Like he didn't believe what they reported."

"Yeah?"

"He said the guy had rig going already."

CHAPTER 34

It was not unusual for him to return to Talbot in the late afternoon. The morning there had gone well enough. The new tech guy, Chris Sebastiene, seemed competent, if a bit too affable. Michael Meacham had come to expect IT staff to be reserved, aloof even. He liked them that way. At five o'clock Ketia left for the day. Chris left shortly thereafter. Melissa White had gone back to Harvard earlier. Now it was just he, the night nurse, and the cleaning lady at the Institute. The five trophy patients and the six subjects were there, but of course Meacham never counted them present.

He surveyed the pharmaceutical supply cabinet with dismay. Next to the saline there remained a limited supply of the solution he had labeled as hypnotic drip. Only he and the chemist Osterman knew what it contained. He needed much more and soon.

Some years back while researching stroke and paralysis he was amazed by some obscure literature he found. There were studies validating that prescription drugs used to treat insomnia were, oddly enough, effective in awakening comatose subjects. Even some patients who had been in coma for years.

He got Osterman to create a cocktail with a derivative of an Amazonian hallucinogen called ayahuasca, sometimes called dead man's vine. He mixed it with the sleep drug zolipidem with amazing results. When the chemist tweaked the formula with a trace of animal tranquilizer and some other additives, Meacham found he could induce waking dreams states in subjects. Unfortunately he accidently killed Arthur Ludlow with an overdose. At least now he knew the tolerance.

He went to his desk and spread out some coke. He remembered recently reading how the Red Sox pitcher Oil Can Boyd revealed that he'd rarely pitched a game not high on cocaine, yet achieved significant success as a major leaguer. No one knew about his habit. Meacham liked Oil Can. Admired him. Meacham had been addicted to coke for so long he lost track of the years. And no one knew. Until now. And now he had a big problem.

*

Chris parked his vehicle at the Adams Inn and walked to the restaurant off the lobby where Ketia waited at a table for two. They left the Institute separately by design. They didn't think it was anybody's business there to know they had begun dating.

"I think I'll get the lobster roll. How about you?" Ketia said.

"Same for me. They make it fresh from the tank."

"I didn't see much of you today. Did you ever make it out of that cave you call the server room?"

"Hardly. When I did, I guess you were over in the other wing."

"So now that you've been at Talbot for a little while, what's your impression?"

"The place is too weird. And Meacham. He's…I dunno."

"Creepy."

"That's it. Talk about a doctor lacking bedside manners."

"You don't need those at Talbot. What else you notice?"

"Someone messes with the back up files. I find them moved. Some of them have been erased. Some altered. Other places I've worked they'd go ape shit if this was happening. I told Meacham. He told me not to worry. I guess no one cares."

"Did you tell Doctor White?"

"No. I don't want to get between those two. I need the work."

"I know what you mean. There's this bag of solution they use with the saline drip in the experimental wing. It's labeled 'hypnotic'. Other places would insist that the chemical content be clearly labeled. I asked Doctor White about it. She said 'that's Doctor Meacham's property'. You're right. I'm not getting in the middle of their issues."

"Know what else is weird," Chris said as the lobster rolls arrived.

"Plenty. But you're new. Try and tell me something I don't already know."

"The night cleaning lady. I know her from the neighborhood. She's a Vodoun priestess, a manbo."

"That I did not know."

CHAPTER 35

"At the risk of re-igniting the Timothy Leary fire at the *Crimson* we are going to discuss wakened dream states today. The most common state is the drug-induced hallucination. Can anyone name another?" Professor White said.

"Trance?" a student called out.

"Excellent. As in the ritual induced or vision quest state."

"Dementia?" Harold said.

"Interesting observation, Harold. It certainly appears in latter stages to be a sort of chronic daydream state. We don't know. The connection between Alzheimer's and dreams is rife for study. Truly an unmined field of research."

"I only ask because I was afraid you might have forgotten it," Harold said.

Professor White ignored the comment. "Any others?" she said.

"Near death?" a student said.

"Absolutely correct. The most powerfully felt dream state. The bright light at the end of the tunnel. The portal to the other world. First we'll consider these states in context of locality. From where do these dream landscapes originate? How can simple…or complex…pharmacology possibly explain them? Where does dream consciousness exist in the physical plane? Then we'll address them from a quantum perspective. How do we see dreams? What light source illuminates them for us? By the way, can anyone tell me where light quanta reside? Better yet, what are light quanta?"

White waited for the response she knew would not come.

"I thought not. But no surprise. Not even Einstein could answer that."

*

Ann Winston stood by the window in her new room looking out at the world and seeing nothing in particular. Meacham and White stood together at her door, observing the observer. Clinically, both were pleased to have another patient with severe dementia in the ward. Meacham was pleased that he successfully revived her from a comatose state. White was particularly pleased because she found the patient's condition fertile ground for her particular research. She wondered how deep did her insanity go. Was she as lost in her dreams as in her waking state? What was the boundary if any? Was she lost at all? Perhaps that was just the perception of the observer.

"Why hasn't the housekeeper emptied the waste basket in here?" Meacham said.

Melissa White said nothing.

"Simple enough task. She missed it two days in a row now. If she can't keep up with it fire her and get somebody else."

White nodded her agreement. Neither took well to being directed. Generally though, White handled personnel matters while Michael Meacham acted as finance officer.

The housekeeper was just coming on shift as Melissa White was preparing to leave for the day. She confronted the employee just outside the server room where Chris Sebastiene was seated with the door open.

"Yveline. You missed the trash again in room six. Please be more attentive."

"Sorry Doctor. Yes. Thank you."

Mellisa walked away as Yveline glanced at Chris, who nodded hello.

"Hello Mister Sebastiene," she said.

"Not Mister Sebastiene," he said. "Chris. I'm Chris, Mrs. Walker. You knew me as a little kid in the neighborhood. I'm the good kid who never taunted you with the mumbo jumbo and witch calls remember? I hauled your trash cans out and shoveled the snow from your sidewalk."

"I remember you Christian."

"You know they'll fire you around here in a minute over a simple trash can don't you?"

"Yes. But I cannot empty that one."

"Why not?"

"That one is cursed. That woman. I cannot go in her room again. There is too much danger. Her soul has been captured. She walks in both worlds."

"You're serious?"

"You know who I am. You know what I am."

Chris knew that some vodoun practitioners could confuse all sorts of physical and mental conditions with curses and hexes. He didn't believe any of it, but was around it all his life.

"I'll empty that trash can for you," he said.

"Thank you Christian," she said.

"Everyday. Before I leave," he said with a wide smile. "But you'll need to get someone else to shovel your snow, Mrs. Walker."

*

"Do you remember Gordon Chamberlain?" Edmund White said, and then took a sip of Glenlivet.

"Of course. Name like that always makes me think of money. Client of yours. Chairman of some Board," said Melissa.

"Retired chairman. Kraft Foods. We spoke today. I think you'll be pleased."

"I'm intrigued."

"Gordon has many causes. The one we spoke about is a man he has looked after financially for many years. An invalid. Gordon pays for his residential care in a facility much like Talbot."

"There is no facility like Talbot."

"You know I'm talking about the normal wing. Anyway, the facility is closing. Gordon inquired as to relocating the patient to Talbot. I ran some figures by him. He didn't blink."

"You are absolutely amazing. I'll call him tomorrow. Ludlow's bed is still warm. This is great!"

"You'll do no such thing. I said you'd connect him with Michael Meacham. You don't want your hands dirtied with financials. Remember?"

"A simple conversation would be harmless enough."

"About a high finance revenue stream?"

"You're right. I'll speak with Michael. Technically we have already filled Ludlow's bed with the new charity subject I told you about, Miss Ann Winston. Shouldn't be any problem moving her over to the experimental wing where she belongs, and doubling up another room. By the way she's out of the coma."

"Isn't that somewhat miraculous?"

"Not in this case. She's gone in and out of coma numerous times. That's half of her life history."

"Did she say anything?"

"Oh sure, but the other half of her history is that she suffers from advanced dementia."

"Well your new patient will provide you ample opportunity for the miraculous."

"How so?"

"Gordon says he holds the Guinness record for longest coma."

CHAPTER 36

Finn rented one of the bays and a lift at the Shell station on Morrissey Boulevard near Neponset Circle. He worked there for the previous owner for years, but the new owner "outsourced" the auto repair service. Now Finn had to pay rent to go to work, and cover his own health benefits.

He was in the bay doing an oil change when he heard a commotion out by the pumps. Loud enough that he could hear it over the constant hip-hop beat that his bay mate always had cranking. Peering over the edge of the bay he saw a twenty-something black male and an older black male wrestling with a sweatshirt-hooded, small-framed black person Finn figured to be a teenage boy. The boy was very agitated and trying to get away. They quickly moved from Finn's view.

"Hey! What are you guys doin'? I'm gonna call the cops," Lenny the station owner yelled at them.

"Call us a cab," one of the men demanded. "We need you to fix our car, and for this we need you to call us a cab."

Finn could see the younger guy speaking as he had come back into view. Apparently the other guy was successful in restraining the teenager. Finn could tell by the cadence that the younger man was Haitian.

The situation had calmed sufficiently that Lenny was doing business with them. Richie, Finn's bay neighbor, climbed back into the bay from which he had jetted out of to help Lenny. Richie was young and brash. Finn thought it wiser to stay in the foxhole and assess before acting.

A cab came and went as Finn finished up the oil change. When he came up and out for air he saw a sedan parked in the lot with a blown radiator steaming. It was a white 2003 Pontiac Vibe.

"Don't see many of these," Lenny said.

"Nope," Finn said. But he was pretty sure he'd seen this one before.

*

Meacham had to place restraints on Sam Stockton. Mellissa White was not pleased but could see no alternative.

"Can't you sedate him?" she said.

"Not without killing him," Meacham said. "With the hypnotic dosage I gave him he would not tolerate sedation."

Disturbing as it was to her, she found the waking trance state Meacham induced in Stockton to be textbook perfect. She almost wished her class could see this. She looked down at Sam whose open eyes travelled wildly in some distant world only he could see. Meacham adjusted the sensors on the subject's head.

"I've been thinking about your work and Sam's dream transcripts, Melissa. I apologize for being dismissive. Jealousy I guess. Let me know if I can assist pulling the data together. Or help in any way. You really should publish you know."

Mellissa White viewed Meacham's conciliatory turn as diversionary and deceitful. She responded by nodding in silence and returning her attention to Stockton.

"Why have you introduced this hypnotic drug, Michael? What is the purpose?"

"I should think it obvious to you. The dream data you reap will be rich."

"Perhaps. But what is your purpose?"

"I believe with the right mixture we might be able to successfully revive patients from coma. There has been some success with similar mixtures. Even with long-term coma. Maybe we could bring back your Guinness record holder there in the other wing. Now wouldn't that be something?"

*

The mother scurried her two small Vietnamese-American children away from the threatening teenager. His black face shrouded in a hoodie, he moved along the inbound train platform at Fields Corner T station crashing into anyone in his erratic path. Noting the development from the outbound side a transit cop called for backup on his radio and raced down the stairs and under the tracks toward the agitator. He emerged just in time to see the teen knock an elderly Asian man onto the tracks. Two young black men bravely jumped down and hurriedly carried the old man toward the stairs at the far end of the platform and away from the arriving train. The hooded teenager pushed away an older man who tried and failed to subdue him. The horn of the arriving train sounded. The transit cop moved toward the agitator as fast as he could. He was still several steps away when the teenager stumbled off the platform and dropped in front of the inbound train.

CHAPTER 37

Meacham's cocaine habit got him into deep debt with the local drug lords. At first he kept cost down by trading the sedating drugs they requested. They asked lots of questions about Talbot. Probing. Trying to find an angle they could exploit. Someone they could extort. They settled on his expertise in chemical control. Reluctantly he would go once each week to a house in Dorchester where a subject was provided. He would demonstrate that he could control the subject by inducing hypnotic trance. Having refined his technique on Ludlow and Stockton, he could now deliver what his creditors wanted. His problem was supply and demand. The chemist, Nils Osterman, could not procure and produce fast enough. The creditors had begun taking the drug from Meacham and administering it on their own to subjects with disastrous results. They still needed him. He wondered for how long. To make matters worse the Herald reporter Dougherty was turning over stones.

Despite his troubles Meacham could still find reward in his work at Talbot. He'd been sincere with Mellissa White about his desire to advance medical science approaches to coma. What she didn't realize was that he was also sincere about attempting to revive the new resident. White would not approve. Experimenting in the residential wing presented legal problems. White would surely find it unethical. Such qualms had not stopped Meacham in the past. He waited until she left for the university before heading over to the residential wing.

Finn called Tony with the plate and VIN from the Vibe. Although the Whitfield Street incident was not necessarily vodoun, it was weird enough that Tony briefed Sean.

Sean and Tony agreed that Finn should fix the Vibe and call when the owner would be picking it up. He did. Sean sat in Tony's unmarked car parked on Morrissey Boulevard with a clear view of the Shell station.

"This must be them," said Tony.

A middle-aged black man, probably one of the trio that dropped the Vibe off, got out of a Honda Pilot and went into the Shell office. The Honda drove off followed by Detective Andrea Coles in her unmarked car. Tony and Sean waited for the man at the Shell to finish his business and retrieve his keys. When he steered the Vibe onto Morrissey they dropped in behind him.

Coles called them with the Codman Square address to which she tailed the Honda. It was a restaurant supply warehouse on New England Avenue. The Honda came back registered to the business.

The Vibe led them to a Washington Street dry cleaner shop, not far from the Square, where they sat in watch.

"Well I guess it's time to hurry up and wait," Tony said. "Mind if I kick Coles loose?"

"Hold off. Bring her over here. Let's see what develops. What you make of this? Dry Cleaner?" Sean said.

"I think they must have jacked up that Whitfield Street dude with some of their fluid."

"Close enough. I looked at the tox report. He had a cocktail of an exotic hallucinogen and sleep med. There were traces of other drugs, the main one typically used to euthanize dogs. Coroner figured that extra treat probably caused the appearance of rigor mortis that he noted at the scene."

"Think I'll stick to beer. Hey. Here comes our Vibe guy."

"Looks like he's upgrading."

They watched the Vibe guy get into an ALL BRIGHT Dry Clean van with ONE HOUR SERVICE panels.

"Coles can take this," Sean said. "Drive us back to the Shell. Let's find out if this guy's repair paperwork is a match to the registered owner of the Vibe," said Sean.

*

Bersconi summoned them on short notice. This time Suzanne Sanchez from Homeland was present. Sean wondered if she even knew they had met previously without her.

"Thank you all for making the time to be here. I know how full your schedules can be," he said.

"I would have made the time last meeting had you asked," Sanchez said.

Bersconi let the remark pass. "There was a suicide at the Fields Corner subway stop yesterday. You are probably thinking so what? Well, we have an agent at Langley who tracks public suicides. All day. Everyday. Nationwide. His program keeps on it while he sleeps. Someone runs in front of a bus in Queens, self-immolates in Berkeley, we take a close look. Suicide-by-cops at LAX or Union Station in D.C., we look. Theory is that terrorist cells do trial runs in crowded places before the big event. We've had five qualifying events in recent weeks. Queens,

Berkeley, Los Angeles, D.C., and our subway jumper. All the bodies are Haitian."

"You think there is any connection…," Sean hesitated. He was going to ask about the missing undercover agent but then remembered that Sanchez had been excluded from the previous need-to-know-only meeting.

"To our missing agent in the Haitian community?" Bersconi said. "Don't worry Sean, I brought Suzanne up to speed."

First names. All friends. A team. This guy is a piece of work, thought Sean.

"We're pulling together the reports, including the coroner's. Preliminary details lead us to believe these are drills. I've asked Suzanne to initiate local precautions. The other cities are on board."

"Why Haitians?" Sean said.

Paul Stearns from the State Department glanced over at Bersconi tacitly seeking permission to speak. "That's what we're hoping you can answer," he said.

CHAPTER 38

Ketia looked all around the Health Center for her class notes. She needed them for her evening class. They weren't in her car so that could only mean she left them in the nurse's office at Talbot after her morning rounds. It took her in the wrong direction and was a hassle, but she drove there to retrieve her notebook.

She was surprised to see Ann Winston's new room in the experimental wing empty as she passed it on her way to the nurse office. A new patient was arriving in the residential wing today so they had moved Miss Winston to experimental. Meacham had to be around. Ketia went to the residential wing to find him.

As she entered the wing a high-pitched scream came from what was Arthur Ludlow's room. Ketia dashed down there and found Ann Winston leaning on a walker. She looked at Ann. Tears rolled down the woman's cheeks. She was pointing to the bed where Meacham was restraining the new patient who appeared to be in some sort of waking trance.

"What are you doing here?" he snapped at Ketia.

Ann screamed again.

"Get her back to her room," he said.

Ketia was glad to have the task. There was something horribly wrong here and she wanted no part of it.

*

The waiter placed some bread on the table along with two glasses of water and hurried off to the next table. Lunchtime at Legal Seafood in Harvard Square was always busy. Mellisa White had asked her husband to meet her there.

"A lunch date. How special. You must have something on your mind," Edmund said.

"I do. I need your advice."

"Attorney client privileged of course. This is about Michael Meacham I presume."

"How do you know?"

"You look troubled. He brings trouble. What's up?"

"Ketia and the new tech guy, Chris Sebastiene, asked to meet with me. They came all the way out here to my Harvard office this morning. Said they didn't want Meacham involved."

"Not surprised. What's he done?"

"For starters he experimented on Gordon's beneficiary."

"I thought he was placed in the residential wing."

"He was. Chris says the night cleaning lady told him she'd seen Meacham experimenting on other residents, including Ludlow. Ketia wants to know what's in the drug he has labeled as hypnotic. She says she cannot provide proper care for patients if she doesn't know their medications."

"It all sounds quite criminal. If that's what you're wanting to hear me say."

"I know. Chris's father is a Boston cop. Ketia knows him and vouches for him. They want to bring him a sample of the drug for testing. Ketia thinks maybe Ludlow should be exhumed and examined for foul play."

"I thought the notice said his services were at a crematorium?"

"I don't recall. Anyway, one step at a time. Do you think I should involve the police?"

"Sounds like it would be unofficial. I'd say it is a good starting point. I mean a Boston cop has no jurisdiction in Quincy. It would be a family favor. A free consultation. Yes. Find out what Meacham is pumping into your charges."

*

Ann Winston's condition was deteriorating rapidly. The inoperable brain tumor continued to grow. Mostly she slept in whatever small comfort the morphine allowed. Doctors Meacham and White stood over her and studied the dream data graphs and charts. Both of them were deeply sheltered in their professional personas and avoiding any confrontation with each other.

"Amazing how it never changes," White said.

"If she is dreaming it would be the same dream over and over of course," Meacham observed.

"I agree. The troubling part is that I've never seen this happen in dementia subjects. Their dream records appear as erratic as their waking states. If anything they dream more than normal subjects. And her waking state is typical enough. Rich with characters only she can see. Do you suppose the tumor is suppressing the dream state?"

"Highly unlikely. I would look to the long states of coma as the cause. Or perhaps a life experience prior to mechanism of injury. Specifically what precipitated her comatose condition?"

"A kick to the head during a high school basketball game. They let her keep playing. She collapsed on her way home. Apparently she was misdiagnosed several times over many months. Seizures. She was institutionalized while still a teenager."

"Unfortunate. She doesn't have much longer you know. Weeks not months at best. Are we making the preparations?"

"Trying. We're having a difficult time finding any next of kin. They seem to have all disappeared. It doesn't help that her name was legally changed to Winston from Connolly in 1970 years after she was institutionalized. Apparently her mother, Irene Connolly, remarried to a Robert Winston when the family relocated from Dorchester to Quincy in 1965. They are both deceased long ago."

They walked to the hall and onto their respective offices without further conversation. Mellisa White studied Ann Winston's dream transcripts at her desk. Too bad she was failing, she thought. She was showing so much promise as a subject. She'd run some of the same scripts and stimuli on her as they had with Sam Stockton. Ann replicated some of the same articulations after waking as did he. Most intriguing how they both became agitated about a "fucking bastard". Ann further described the character as "that skinny bastard."

"Melissa you're going to want to see this," Meacham said from White's office doorway.

Melissa followed him to the new wing where their newest resident lay sideways in bed. His eyes were open and tracking them as they entered the room.

"He'll never move or speak, and he is no doubt totally insane, but you can close the book on that Guinness record now," Meacham said.

CHAPTER 39

The boy looked to be about twelve but he weighed less than most ten year olds. He came to the Health Center by himself. The front desk was unable to determine why. The only English word he had spoken so far was help.

"I am Ketia. You?" she said mostly with gestures.

"Ali," he said.

"Where is home?"

"Mali."

Ketia thought he might have pointed in a general direction out the window toward the neighborhood surrounding Codman Square. But Mali? Ivory Coast of Africa. What is this child doing here? His cadence suggested a West African dialect. She knew that French was the official language of Mali so she tried speaking to him in Kreyol with some success. Before she called child protective service she stepped out front and asked Tony to please come to her office for a minute. She told him about the boy as they walked.

"And he told me how he was approached by a man when he was eleven and offered one-hundred dollars if he would work for a year at the cacao plantation," Ketia said.

"That would be a fortune in Mali," Tony said.

"Except he never got a dime. All he ever got was whipped with a cacao branch if he didn't gather beans fast enough."

"I'd heard that chocolate was largely produced with slave labor."

"And you know what? The kid doesn't even know what chocolate is!"

"So where is this young man?" Tony said.

"He went to the restroom."

"Kid's his age are usually pretty quick about that business. Let me check."

In less than a minute Tony returned.

"He's gone," he said.

From the Health Center steps Codman Square presented Ketia six options. She immediately discounted heading either way on Washington Street because it was mostly commercial. Going down Centre Street or Talbot Avenue toward Ashmont led away from the poverty from which Ali most certainly had come. Her choice was between taking Talbot Avenue toward the projects or Norfolk Street. She chose Norfolk, the old Indian trail. She hurried passed Whitfield Street and the Taste of Jamaica restaurant. Approaching the graveyard and Codman's tomb she still could not see him. Then she saw him near the old building Tony always called

Saint Matthew's little school, although it had not functioned as that for forty years. By the time she reached it Ali was three blocks ahead of her on Norfolk by Ferndale Street. Moving as quickly as she could, she saw him about to turn down New England Avenue. She was still in shouting range.

"Ali! Ali! Stop. Wait for me," she called out.

Ali turned and looked back at her but did not wait. When she got to New England Avenue she gave up. Ali was out of sight and she did not feel comfortable venturing along the street full of abandoned warehouses.

CHAPTER 40

As a reporter Dougherty had friends on the streets. Friends in the shadows. He found out that Meacham visited a certain house on Whitfield Street each week at the same time. He heard rumors of vodoun activity at the premises. He knew a man died out front under mysterious circumstances. His friend in the coroner's office leaked him the toxicology report. Even more interesting, his friend told him that the teenager who got crushed under a train at Fields Corner had the same crap in his system.

When he'd followed Doctor Michael Meacham to the two-family house in Cambridge, he saw a guy come out right after Meacham went in. The man was carrying an aluminum medical case. The case seemed an odd fit to the locale so he decided to follow his car. The guy got out at the Best Western in Allston.

Later, he researched the occupants of the Cambridge two-family. An elderly couple lived downstairs. Chemist upstairs. Dougherty figured Meacham frequented the upstairs. He figured the aluminum case guy did also. And he was sure he'd witnessed a drug deal at the locks.

He couldn't figure out Melissa White's role, and where the dream stuff fit in. Maybe it didn't. Either way he intended to find out. He followed White from the Professor's office to a restaurant bar in Harvard Square called the *Casablanca*.

White went to the bar. Dougherty recognized the bartender and ducked back outside to avoid being revealed. At the curb two men made it apparent to him that he was not the only one playing this game. They showed him their FBI badges and escorted him away for questioning.

Melissa White agreed to meet Sean Leahy in Harvard Square at four thirty downstairs at

Casablanca. She arrived early and ordered a glass of wine. Class was finished for the day, and this was her favorite after work spot. She was nervous because she didn't know what kind of problem Leahy would present. She did not want cops involved. Especially not this guy, from some police intelligence network with reach to the FBI.

"Here you go Professor," said Jorge the bartender as he delivered the wine. Jorge considered himself a skilled bartender. He sensed the edge in his patron and tried to put her at ease. "Other day I leaned over the bar and said 'We don't allow no faster-than-light neutrinos in here man'," Jorge paused and looked at White. "A neutrino walks into the bar."

White shook her head and took a sip. "I guess it's appropriate that I laughed at that joke before you even told it. Like last year. That's a stale one Jorge."

"Oh well. Got you out of your funk anyway. Say you still have that psychiatrist business associate of yours, Professor?"

"Michael Meacham? Yes, but he's not a psychiatrist."

"Weird dude nonetheless. He was in here the other day and this reporter, from the Herald I think, was all over him."

"What did you hear?"

"Nothin' much. Happened fast. Got heated. They left."

White turned her attention back to her glass.

"Professor, you know when I was a kid growing up in Mexico, I had some troubles. My parents had some money so they sent me to a psychiatrist to get my head straight, you know. So I went to see this doctor in Mexico City for about five years. On my last session he told me something that made me cry."

Melissa thought Jorge was Puerto Rican, not Mexican, but she was intrigued. "What he say?"

"No habla espanol," Jorge grinned and winked. Then he went off to attend to other patrons.

Sean Leahy walked up and introduced himself to the Professor.

"The drug your associate possesses is an exotic concoction. It was in the systems of two victims who died in mysterious circumstances recently. Sergeant Sebastiene was obligated to inform me. Ketia is a friend. She thinks highly of you. I need you to help with the investigation," Sean said from his seat next to Melissa White at the corner table they had moved to from the bar.

"Murder? My God!"

"I didn't say that. Could be. I'd like you to call Sergeant Sebastiene anytime your associate leaves the Institute. By the time his vehicle reaches Quincy Shore Drive we'll have a tail on him. We're going to find out what activities he has going on."

"Absolutely. Anything I can do to help."

"There's more. Monitor this drug supply. Anymore comes in. Any leaves. Let us know."

"Are we ...is the Institute ... in trouble?" Melissa said, trying not to sound guilty but failing.

"Possibly. If I were you I'd take every possible precaution to protect the well being of your clients. Legally there is nothing we can do at this point. They are all Doctor Meacham's patients. If you, or Ketia, suspect he is harming any of them, we can act. Ketia told us about the death of an Arthur Ludlow. We looked into it. Meacham signed the death certificate as natural causes. The body was cremated. So that ... pardon the expression... is a dead end."

CHAPTER 41

Tony got a call from Melissa White saying Meacham was moving a supply of the drug out of Talbot Institute. Working cooperatively with the State Police he picked up Meacham's car in his unmarked cruiser and was several car-lengths behind him on Gallivan Boulevard.

Meacham turned on Washington Street and was headed toward Codman Square when he abruptly turned right on Fuller Street, parked and exited. Tony parked and followed on foot as Meacham carried a package to a vacant plumbing supply store on Washington. Someone answered his knock and he disappeared into the windowless warehouse.

Tony returned to his vehicle and re-positioned it to a good vantage point. After fifteen minutes Meacham came out empty handed and headed back to his car. Tony let him go. He wanted to see where the drugs were going.

Nils rented space for his lab in an industrial park near Fresh Pond. Aside from his hobby of tinkering with aromas, the Inman Square home office was free of chemicals. This no doubt frustrated the two FBI agents who dropped in on him. One stood stoically watching from a vantage point where he could see the hall leading to the other rooms of the flat. The other sat comfortably at the kitchen table with Nils, who he chatted up like an old friend.

"So you got this lab nearby where you make the cocktail for Doctor Meacham?"

"Correct. Well actually I make it under contract for the Talbot Institute."

"We might need to get over to your lab. Cross the t's dot the i's. You know. Of course we'd get a warrant."

"Of course." Nils knew they were fishing. The agent was dancing all around, but what he wanted was something on Meacham. Something the agent didn't know but figured Nils did. Nils decided to play into it and draw him out.

"Meacham ever mention why he needed your services?"

"He uses the hypnotic in dream research."

"He say why he does the research?"

"I never asked. I would expect for admirable scientific purposes."

"You think a teenager zonked on your cocktail then crushed by a train is admirable?"

"I don't know what you are talking about."

"We think this teenager was part of Meacham's research. We think Meacham might try something like this again. Something bigger. If he does I wouldn't want to be you. Unless of course you're helping us stop him."

"Are you asking me to cease my contractual work?"

"We're asking you to work with us. He ever mention anything about having the subway be part of his experiments?"

Nils saw this as his big chance. He needed to buy time. Needed a distraction. These guys could close in on him fast. Shutting down his off-shore operation would ruin him. But the work he did on some of his other contracts would put him in jail.

"Well not exactly, but…" Nils reached for some of the water he had boiled for coffee. He pushed a small bowl toward the agent. "He does have me prepare aromas from time to time. I gather there is an olfactory stimulus involved in his research. Here. Smell this. Meacham asked me to make it for him."

The agents made eye contact. The one standing visibly tensed. The one seated considered the steaming bowl then put his nose to the vapors.

"Smells like the subway," he said signaling the standing agent to come have a whiff, which he did.

"We'd like to take a sample of this with us."

"Absolutely."

Nils packaged the sample for them while the agent in the chair asked a few more leading questions. Nils fabricated answers that seemed to please the agent.

"We'll be in touch," the speaking agent said as they left.

First Nils booked a flight to Sweden. Then he left to go clean out his lab.

Tony recognized the man who exited the Washington Street plumbing supply store and watched as he got into a familiar Pontiac Vibe. He followed the Vibe to Whitfield Street. The driver got out carrying the package Meacham had delivered. Tony presumed it contained the hypnotic drug. The owner of the Vibe, and the guy he previously witnessed driving the ALL BRIGHT Dry Clean van, were the one and same Robert Lucas. The vehicle was registered to Lucas at the Whitfield Street address where he and Finn got stumbled into by a dead guy. The same address Lucas just entered.

Tony called Coles and additional back up to wait with him. After about thirty minutes Lucas and his companion from the Shell station came out with a black woman about thirty wearing a tight short skirt, and a teenage boy in a hooded sweatshirt. The woman and boy looked enough alike to be mother and son. They also stumbled like the dead guy, only they kept living. Supported by Lucas and his buddy they were escorted to the Vibe and placed in the back.

Tony had enough. Before the men could get into the Vibe, he signaled for his team to move in and arrest them. He'd book them on suspicion. The District Attorney could sort out whether kidnapping, murder or both charges would stick. He got an ambulance rolling for the woman and the teen, who appeared to both be locked in a mindless drug-induced trance.

"Police. Raise your hands slowly. You are under arrest. Don't move," said Coles as her two back up officers quickly moved in and put the men in cuffs. The moment that was done and Coles holstered her weapon a trio of men swooped in from the shadows.

"FBI," said the leader holding his badge high.

"These guys are ours. Federal jurisdiction. Murder of a federal agent."

"Nice coordination boys," Tony said sarcastically. When his anger subsided enough so he could speak, he called Sean Leahy.

CHAPTER 42

The tension in the room was not going to be eased by pleasant words so none were heard. This was not a team. It was two. Sean sat on one side of the table with Suzanne Sanchez. Paul Stearns sat on the other with Bersconi who naturally assumed command.

"You asked us for help and all the while you run a shadow operation around us. Why waste our time?" Sean said.

"A federal agent was missing. Had in fact been killed. We did what was necessary," Bersconi said.

"You knew he was dead. You knew who did it. We were not informed. You played us. In fact you placed my team in danger unnecessarily," Sean said.

"You and I can pick up that conversation after we finish here. The reason I called you all…" Bersconi said.

"I was coming to see you anyway," Sean interrupted.

"The reason for this meeting is to inform you that we have substantial evidence of a terrorist attack on the Boston subway. Possibly as soon as this week."

"And this evidence is?" Sanchez said.

"Sources are still developing. We'll let you know the full details when we can. I assure you what we have is credible. We need you to place your resources on full alert."

"None of the Homeland staff in the cities that you wanted alerted found any evidence of suicide drills, or national coordination of terrorist activity within their respective Haitian communities," Sanchez said.

"Apparently they didn't look in the right places. We'll have a briefing paper delivered to all of you personally this afternoon. Thank you for coming in," Bersconi said.

"Thank you Neil," Paul Stearns said as he nodded to the others and left.

Suzanne Sanchez glanced at an unmoving Sean and a stone-faced Bersconi. With an audible sigh she stood and left with the body language of displeasure.

"You were saying," Sean said as soon as Suzanne was out the door.

"Certain developments raised suspicions early on. We had to be sure that no one inside your ranks was complicit," Bersconi said.

"Outrageous. What are you talking about?"

"We find our guy in the morgue. Delivered there by your Sergeant and his long-lost pal, who happens to be your father. Cause of death is a cocktail of exotic drugs from a hinky Institute where your

Sergeant's son is employed with his new girlfriend, who also happens to be dating you. See where I'm going with this?"

"Yeah. You're taking a string of coincidences and half-truths and writing an implausible movie script."

"Just following all the leads. Relax. You come up clear. Now we need to move on to the impending threat. I'll need you to…"

"The City has no information at this time from any source of any threat to public safety."

"You are treading into dangerous water Leahy. Impeding a federal investigation. Obstruction of justice."

"I look forward to reviewing your briefing paper. Get it to me as soon as possible Special Agent." Sean said as he stood. "Have a good day."

*

The FBI briefing paper did not reveal sources by name. The credible evidence centered on a drug dealer who provided the hypnotic drug, and a profile developed from several incidents indicating that the attack would come from a male Haitian teenager, most likely on the transit Red Line. The suspect would be under hypnotic trance, and would attempt to disperse a biological weapon into the rush hour subway commuter population. The Center for Disease Control provided an addendum on a mutation from avian flu as the most likely substance to be used.

Sean knew the profile leaned heavily on three teenagers. The one hospitalized from Whitfield Street last night. The one reported at the Shell station. The one killed by the train. The briefing paper referenced supporting intelligence from other cities. But without the unidentified drug dealer's information Sean did not find the threat credible.

After briefing the Mayor and Police Commissioner, he walked through the ornate bronze hallway to the small conference room he had reserved.

"Hello again Suzanne," Sean said as he closed the conference room door.

The room was soundproofed. A glass wall somewhat compromised privacy. Sean sometimes used this room when he met alone with a female. Trading some privacy for protection against possible false accusations of improper behavior was standard practice. His female colleagues took the same precaution when meeting solo with a male. Sean thought it was all a bit paranoid. Sexist even. He had no qualms about being in a closed room with Suzanne Sanchez.

"Nice room Leahy. Are you planning on interrogating me or just afraid I might jump you?" Suzanne said.

"This is the only room available."

"We have one just like it. Probably designed by a lawyer. Thank you for seeing me on short notice

Sean. I assume you've received and considered the FBI brief?" Suzanne said.

"Yes. Matter of fact I just briefed the Mayor."

"What did he think?"

"He mumbled something about not wanting to have another false bomb-threat embarrassment, like the gadget marketing in 2007 that put traffic on our roads and bridges in gridlock. Basically we agreed to avoid being obstructionist and cooperate just enough to assure the FBI gets all the credit, or all the blame."

"Exactly our position."

"I think they can't see the forest for the trees."

"They do seem myopic. Also I'm confused that when you asked 'Why Haitians?' they punted back to you."

"Bersconi badly wants the big collar that will propel him to Washington. He allows poorly sampled stats and false assumptions to move him forward. I think Stearns is being less than forthright. State Department must have some intelligence from the Embassy in Haiti or elsewhere. The only terror we can find here is the poverty level in our Haitian community. There are no dots connecting an attack to the subway or any urban center."

"When we alerted the Homeland centers in the other cities, they said the same thing," Suzanne said.

"You had enough of your office for today, Suzanne?"

"Easily. What do you have in mind?"

"Let's take a ride around Dorchester," Sean said.

"How romantic."

*

Sean and Suzanne Sanchez drove first to the ALL BRIGHT Dry Cleaner on Washington, then to the Restaurant Supply on New England Avenue. Sean explained how the guys taken last night by the FBI had previously been tailed to both places. Then they drove on.

"This is the place where the drug supply was delivered," said Sean as he pointed out the vacant plumbing warehouse on Washington Street.

"I know you're going to thread these three places together for me somehow beyond the obvious," Suzanne said. She would have been less diplomatic with most men. She liked Sean.

"Alright. So here it is. I went to our performance measurement guy. His shop has all the numbers. I asked him to give me a grid on Codman Square with all the blighted properties plotted over all the food and drink establishments with poor health code ratings, and all the police reports on prostitution."

"Nice mix," Suzanne said.

"We also looked at immigration data and child abuse incidents. This guy we busted last night, Lucas, owns the Dry Cleaner and also an interest in the restaurant supply. The data and the grid show overlapping hot spots in the triangle between the three places I just showed you. And that includes the Whitfield Street place where the bust went down and the FBI agent died."

"I'm still confused but I can see why the FBI would be interested."

"Of course. That's the obvious. They see the trees. But the forest requires a better vantage point."

"I get it. Prostitution. Labor in the scrub kitchens. Children. Undocumented immigrants. This is the stronghold of a contemporary slavery ring. They're operating right in front of us yet they're practically invisible," Suzanne said.

"They get moved in and through here like the coyotes move their Mexican clients across the desert borders. Difference being the Mexicans are seeking a better life. These poor souls get dispersed to urban hells from here to Chicago with no chance of ever being free."

"How did you know to look?"

"It's the drugging that revealed them. They tried to hide it by masking it in the surrounding Vodoun culture. They even had the neighborhood fooled."

"So the trance keeps their captives compliant. And it's easier to bring them out of it than with hard drugs or sedatives when their services are needed," Suzanne said.

"Or when a slave buyer comes shopping. Know what I'm thinking Suzanne?"

"That I should contact New York, California, Washington D.C., all the other Haitian population centers and have them start looking for a forest."

CHAPTER 43

Thomas was not his real name but he was getting used to it. The chemist had to call him something. Thomas thought the chemist had been careless letting the guy named Michael into the kitchen while he was still there with the product. That mistake led the FBI to the chemist and put the entire operation in jeopardy. Thomas thought it good that the chemist flee to Sweden. With the final batch of the virus waiting at the lab this could still work out, he told himself. But the Michael guy presents a problem. And the problem would follow the chemist to Sweden. But the chemist is a bright guy. He proposed a solution that Thomas liked. And he might need the chemist later. The Michael guy would need to be dispatched. The reporter also. That fool followed him to the hotel and sat in the parking lot long enough to give Leon time to get the car from out back and follow the stupid bastard to the newspaper office. Regardless, another problem. Three problems actually when you count Lucas. The FBI busted Lucas but the judge threw out the charges for lack of evidence. He'd need to get to Lucas while he was still sprung. Same solution.

*

"Hello Doctor Meacham. This is Thomas. We met briefly in Nils Osterman's kitchen."

"I can't say that I recall," Meacham lied into the speakerphone on his desk.

"No matter. Nils is socially inept. He obviously neglected to tell you that I am his business partner. Nils had to leave town. He left a shipment of the ayahuasca preparation for you to pick up."

"How strange. We had not discussed this at all."

"Well I can't exactly return it. Are you not interested?

"No. No. I mean of course I am interested."

"Excellent. I will call you back with details on when and where as soon as I can. Good day."

Meacham stared at his silent phone. Unsettled he reached for his bindle of cocaine.

*

Thomas entered the warehouse on New England Avenue expecting to find Lucas alone as he had arranged. Instead he found two other men there loading children into a van. One climbed into the driver seat of the loaded van and drove out onto the street and away. The other man closed the bay door.

Six or seven children remained sprawled on the filthy floor. The man brought them water.

"Lucas. What the fuck?" Thomas said.

"Sorry Thomas. Unexpected buyer from Philadelphia. We had to herd them together quickly."

Thomas studied the room. The children were anywhere from eight to about twelve. All boys. Probably Somalian. They were all zonked on the drug that killed the FBI spy. There was shit and puke everywhere. "Don't you clean them up before delivery?"

Lucas didn't answer. Thomas could care less. He didn't traffic humans. Weapons and drugs were his trade. The assault weapons he sent to Somalia in exchange for fuel rods travelled the same tanker routes as these kids. Boys and women were Lucas's business. In addition to his human trade, Lucas ran drugs in Dorchester. Lucas had put him in touch with Osterman, the chemist Thomas greatly needed.

Thomas's main trade was in Queens where he supplied drugs to the large Haitian population. His new client wanted a biological weapon delivered to an Islamic extremist cell in Brooklyn. The federal agents that infiltrated Lucas's operation in Codman Square had figured out too much of what Thomas was up to. Lucas and he had to take them out.

"Lucas call your friend over here for a minute will you?"

Lucas pulled the guy away from his task and walked over with him to Thomas.

Thomas quickly put a round into the center of each of their foreheads and walked out of the warehouse.

*

Sometimes she picked up cans and bottles as she walked about. She heard two gunshots come from inside the warehouse. The man barely noticed her as he came out and walked past her to a vehicle parked on New England Avenue. She picked the can from the gutter and added it to her bag. Her old eyes strained to see the letters and numbers as the car sped away. She spoke them to herself and moved on toward the bus stop.

CHAPTER 44

Tony pulled his patrol car to the curb at the apartment building on Adams Street. Finn climbed in.

"Whatta the neighbors gonna think?"

"Probably say there goes the neighborhood," Tony said. "Black cop arrestin' you. Remember to bring the box?"

"Ain't that what this is all about?"

"Just checking. A curator named Rawlings gonna meet with us at the museum. Said he could run the box under a scanner like you asked."

"Great. Damn box been haunting me all my life. Glad to be rid of it, but it'd be nice to know what's in it first."

Rawlings met them at the front desk of the Museum of Fine Arts. He was a typical curator. Thin. Thick eyeglasses. Tweed jacket. Bow tie. He looked to be thirty-something going on sixty.

"Pleased to meet you, Officer Sebastiene and Mr.?"

"Leahy. Finn Leahy."

Rawlings shook their hands. "I am so excited about the missing box. Please, let's go to my office. There is some paperwork. And then we'll do the scan."

They followed him to a small office with a desk and just enough chairs to accommodate them. A three-foot square crate sat on a nearby table.

"Okay. Paperwork. As I told the Officer, the box you have belongs to this crate of artifacts. Well, junk actually, that the museum has held onto for ages and…"

"Since we were kids," interjected Finn.

"But he doesn't need to know that part," Tony said.

"...we are relieved that you have found the heirs to the donor so we can finally return the items," Rawlings continued undaunted as he slid a stack of documents to Tony.

"Actually, Mr. Leahy and I are still searching for the family," said Tony.

"May I..." said Rawlings retrieving the unsigned documents, "...see the box?"

Finn handed him the box.

"Thank you," said Rawlings. "Most interesting. Clearly of West African origin. See these markings. And the weave. It is made of branches. That is why it appears to have no way to be opened. Good craftsmanship. Unlike the other items, this is museum quality. How...? Sorry, the Officer suggested, and I agreed, that it is probably most expeditious that we not inquire as to how you came into possession of the box. Now if you could just find someone to sign these deaccessioning papers I have authorized, the museum will have no further interest."

"Can we scan the box now Mr. Rawlings?" Finn said.

"One more thing. This is quite important. Ah, the reason why we held onto these items so long."

Rawlings removed a framed picture of a middle-aged African-American woman taken in front of a Dorchester style three decker house with a 1950's Studebaker parked on the street.

"You see what I see," Tony said, his eyes as wide as the night Finn went into the tomb.

"Excuse me Mr. Rawlings," Finn said as he directed his full attention to Tony. "The fuckin'…"

"…Talbot Avenue witch!" Tony finished.

*

Rawlings related how the record on the crate showed that museum staff had accepted it in error back in 1965, and repeatedly attempted to return the items to the owner of record. The owner turned out to be a resident of the Mattapan Hospital for the Insane, and no next of kin could be readily located. After awhile the box was relegated to the archive of useless things. When he took over as curator Rawlings went about cleaning up the archives and had staff go through each item meticulously.

"There was an unrecorded item housed in the frame behind this picture," Rawlings said as he held up a single sheet of paper. He was wearing latex gloves and signaled with his eyes that Finn and Tony should each put on a pair from the nearby box. They did.

Tony studied the document through the protective sheath in which Rawlings had encased it. "AGREEMENT OF LIMITED PARTNERSHIP, dated 1780 and signed by Dr. James Baker and Nathaniel Blake," he read aloud and handed it to Finn.

"Such share of interest as certificate holds I hereby transfer to Katherine Preston," Finn read.

"That's hand written on the bottom and signed again by Blake, dated 1803."

"I might well have signed an authorization for destruction of the entire crate and contents were it not for that document," Rawlings said. "Much as I'd like to exhibit it, I believe it might be of some actual value to whomever it is entitled."

"We'll do our best to find out," Tony said.

"Now can we scan that box?" Finn said.

They went to an open space in a warehouse part of the complex where Rawlings placed the box in a machine that looked part airport security, part tanning booth. He pressed a button and looked at a screen.

"Empty," he said.

CHAPTER 45

Tony liked to check in with Chris at least once a month over an after work beer at the Ashmont Grille. He was pleasantly surprised to see Ketia accompanying his son to their ritual.

"I'm glad to see you two finally bumped into each other," Tony said.

"We work together, Tony," Ketia said.

"Had the same work schedule today so I invited Ketia to join us," Chris said in father-son code Tony heard as 'No further explanation required.'

"Hey, well nice coordination. So how'd the day go at the Institute? Wait. I ordered a Red Stripe. What can I get for you two?" Tony said, addressing the question to Ketia first then Chris with his eyes.

"Red Stripe is fine for me," she said.

"Same here," Chris said.

Tony placed the order and returned to his question. "The Institute?"

"You probably went to see Sean?" Ketia said.

"I sure did," Tony said with a chuckle. "I sure do."

"Things have gotten real tense between White and Meacham. They avoid each other it seems," Ketia said.

"Another weird thing. You remember Mrs. Walker, Dad?"

"Yveline Walker. Yes. She doesn't much care for my uniform I guess. She hasn't acknowledged me for years."

"Well she does evening clean up at Talbot. You know she is a practicing vodoun priestess?"

"I recall. You know the funny thing about those folks is that the most highly respected within their circle are practically invisible outside of it. They can be cutting your hair or taking out your trash. You'd never know how much personal power they carry."

"Well she came up short on the power thing at Talbot and I saved her job for her."

"So she owes you does she?" Tony said.

"I guess you could say that, but I hadn't thought of it that way."

"Reason I say that is … well," Tony hesitated.

Ketia read him perfectly. "Tony, you can't always be the one doing everything for everybody else. You need a favor? Ask," Ketia said.

"What do you need Dad?" Chris said.

"Could you ask Mrs. Walker to meet with me? Tell her it is not police work. It is a neighborhood thing. Personal. Tell her I have something that someone lost."

*

Yveline Walker answered the door knock at her Ferndale Street flat to see Tony arriving as expected for the meeting she had agreed to with him.

"Officer Sebastiene. Come in. But please. One more time. Are you sure this is not police work?"

Tony was dressed in civilian casual clothes. "Mrs. Walker. I assure you. This actually has to do with when we were kids in the neighborhood here. And please, call me Tony."

"Very well then. When we were young I was Yveline. Still am if you please. Despite how I may appear, I still feel young," she said leading him to a soft chair in the parlor.

A bead curtain separated the parlor from a den. From where he sat Tony could look through some of the strands and see candles burning on an altar adorned with many objects.

"So how can I help you, Tony?"

"Mrs.…Yveline, when I was a boy there was an old woman living on Talbot Avenue we used to taunt," said Tony. He had difficulty calling her Yveline because she would have been in her mid twenties back then. Too old for him to associate with. He'd always known her as Mrs. Walker.

"You called her the witch."

"You know of her then?"

"I was at her house once when you boys were taunting. My mother and I looked in on her from time to time for a family friend who was her niece."

"Can you put me in touch with the niece?"

"Why, may I ask?"

"As I mentioned on the phone, a boyhood friend came upon a possession of hers he wishes to return. There is paperwork involved only an heir can complete."

"Please describe the possession for me."

Tony described the box as well as Finn's nightmares.

"Your friend is in possession of a powerful object. It was not meant that he have this. I cannot guess its purpose but you are correct in trying to return it."

"So will you put me in touch with the niece?"

"She has passed."

"Do you remember her name?"

"Yes but I think you'd rather have the name of her daughter who volunteers at the Health Center. Sheila Waters. Do you know her?"

"Sheila. Of course. I'll be darned. Thank you Yveline."

"Glad I could help. And I am so glad you weren't here officially. I am so sick of the police."

Tony knew of no police activity at this address.

"Have the police been to see you?"

"Yes…" she said as a teenage boy pushed through the bead curtain. "And my great nephew here as well."

"Sorry Aunt Yveline," said the boy as he disappeared back through the curtain.

"FBI," she continued. "All kinds of ridiculous questions."

"What do they want?"

"They think we may know something about the death of one of their agents."

"Do you?"

"Tony. Let me tell you something about my true work. You can see the altar in there. Most folks think being a priestess is all about spells and cures and trances. The real work is in the discipline. It takes skill to slow time down and truly see what is hiding between the cracks. The same skill allows one to move through the cracks almost unseen. I have seen things the FBI should want to see. But they are blind and disinterested. What they are looking for is not there."

"Yes. But you didn't answer my question."

"There are some very bad people out there. Right here in this neighborhood. I see them but they do not see me."

"Would you show me where?"

Yveline hesitated before speaking. "Yes. I will. But not for the police. I will do this for you Tony. And for your friend who carries a piece from the past toward a future in search of the present. Such a talisman may prove fortuitous for us all."

Taking every precaution to assuage Yveline Walker's disdain of police, Tony picked her up in his personal vehicle on his day off. He drove her down Ferndale Street to Southern Avenue as she requested.

"A mother brought me a boy who could not speak," she said handing him a slip of paper. "Drive us along New England Avenue," she said.

"There," she said pointing out the restaurant supply warehouse matching the address on the slip of paper Tony held. "I could not help the boy. The mother gave me that slip of paper. It is where they were held captive. They were African. They did not belong here. I tried to help them escape."

"There is more written on the paper. Looks like a partial plate number XLB 7_?"

"I added that just recently. It is from the vehicle of a man I saw leaving the place. I could not read all the numbers. There were gunshots. Now take us up Talbot Avenue," she said. "And down Whitfield Street." She pointed out several more properties all along the route and told of what she had observed.

"Thank you Yveline. This is all most helpful," Tony said.

"You may take me for coffee now," Yveline said.

CHAPTER 46

The four of them sat at the conference table in Fields Corner Police Station. At Sean's request Lt. Mooney attended the briefing given by Tony with his partner Detective Andrea Coles. The pair had done some preliminary investigation following up on the information provided by Yveline Walker.

"There is a prostitution ring housed on New England Avenue. There doesn't appear to be any activity there or nearby. Two of the blighted three deckers are a base of operations," Tony said.

"A dormitory of sorts. Or more like a concentration camp," Coles said.

"As you know we found the bodies of Robert Lucas and a John Doe at the restaurant supply warehouse on New England Avenue. John Doe's head was a mess but he probably is the same guy Andrea followed there the day Sean and I tracked Lucas and his Vibe from the Shell. All the warehouses by the tracks need a closer look," Tony said.

"There are also several blighted residences along Talbot Avenue that have highly transient tenants," Coles said.

"One in particular has a number of teenage boys. Mrs. Walker says she is sure boys are carefully rotated in and out," Tony said.

Sean looked at Lt. Mooney. "Tim you can see we have something here. The sergeant and the detective have turned over the stones. I will provide you the grid developed by City Hall. I think we need to redirect some of your personnel. I can bring in any specialists you may need. And you should have someone talk with that Herald reporter, Dougherty. Find out how he knows so much. And what more he knows."

"FBI still involved?" Mooney said.

"Not with us. We're taking a fork in the road," Sean said.

"Good. Didn't appreciate the way they stepped on our guys."

"Neither did I. Or the Mayor for that matter."

"One more thing," said Tony. "Mrs. Walker said some of the recent Haitian immigrants speak of strangers who walk in trance. They were afraid so would not tell her much. From what she could gather these strangers were non-Haitians. Somalian maybe or West African. She never saw any herself, other than the mother and boy she sheltered, so she couldn't be sure."

"Like they were invisible," Sean said.

*

Dougherty considered Detective Cole's question and wondered if he should insulate himself with freedom of the press rights. He decided to answer.

"Yes I spoke with the FBI. I felt intimidated. I could have objected but I figured the story might be better if I just followed where it led."

"And you told them what you just told me about following Meacham to the chemist's flat in Cambridge?" Coles said.

"Yes and about tailing the guy who came out with the aluminum case to the Allston Best Western."

"May I have the make, model and plate number of the vehicle you followed to the hotel?"

"I don't see why not. I already gave it to the FBI."

"Why did you start following Meacham in the first place?"

"I saw the media splash about Professor Melissa White's kooky Harvard class. That led me to the Talbot Institute and Meacham. I picked up some buzz about the place while working my Dorchester news beat. So I started nosing around."

"Where's the story going Mr. Dougherty?"

"You tell me Detective and I'll be glad to wrap it up in the morning edition."

*

Detective Coles traced the vehicle Dougherty had followed. It belonged to a rental company. The vehicle had been returned. The lessee, Thomas Reid, was a fictitious person. Coles was pondering this dead end when her cell rang.

"Detective Coles? This is Dougherty. I need your help."

"Slow down Dougherty. Easy. What's wrong?"

"The guy I tailed to the hotel just called. Thomas. He said I needed to meet him. Said he had a story for me I would want. Wouldn't tell me what it was about. I…I think I'm being set up."

"Why do you say that?"

"Look. I've been at this game a long time. I'm usually right on hunches. This smells bad."

"How did he introduce himself on the phone?"

"He said, 'this is Thomas the guy you followed to the motel'. Why?"

"Because I gotta wonder how he found you. Listen Dougherty. You're not the top of the food chain in this sleuthing business. He must have had an associate on your tail. When are you supposed to meet with him?"

"He's gonna call back. You're probably right. When I left that hotel I must have been followed. That's how they found me of course. On the way home I stopped at a gas station. I noticed a car pull up short at the curb. It started up again when I did. I drove to the office instead of going home."

"Did you get the plate number?"

"No."

"Make and model?"

"Nissan Altima. Silver"

"OK. Call me when this guy Thomas calls you back. We'll cover you."

"Thank you Detective Coles."

"Not a problem. Top of the food chain you know. Meanwhile lay low and stop following people around."

CHAPTER 47

"You have to be brave. Go. Pick up the package," his Aunt Yveline told him.

At first he felt the old fear. Gradually he grew braver as he distanced his aunt's house on Ferndale and approached the place where the package awaited. He walked past the old church and People's Market along Washington Street into the late afternoon sun with Codman Square behind him. But then he started feeling lightheaded and disoriented. Finally he got to his destination. He entered ALL BRIGHT Dry Cleaners and was given the package. It was a little larger than a manila envelope and wrapped tightly with plastic. After he exited the shop he stuck it up inside the front of his hooded sweatshirt. He began to feel better. Adventurous even. He turned on Park Street and walked down the hill to Fields Corner.

*

"He's coming out," the agent said into a radio microphone from a concealed vantage point. "He stuck a package up the front of a hooded sweatshirt."

"We're in position at Fields Corner," a voice from the radio replied.

"He's turned down Park Street. Looks like he's coming to you."

"We're ready. There could be others. Dispatch advises that we are now on condition red," the radio voice said.

*

He figured his aunt would be proud of him. He walked past a place called the Blarney Stone and saw pool tables inside. This stretch of Dorchester Avenue was all new to him. He heard a rumble and looked up to see a subway train cross the elevated track over the street just ahead. Suddenly he started to feel really bad and worried for no reason. He broke out in a cold sweat. He felt chilled so he pulled the hood over his head. He went into a trance, trembled and almost fell down. It passed. His head cleared. Then he noticed the two men approaching him. One reached out to grab him. He squirmed, turned and ran toward the subway station. The package slid out. He caught it in full stride and tucked it like a football. When he got to the train ramp he ran up it as fast as he could. He saw a Transit cop up ahead. He ran toward the cop. The cop drew his weapon and pointed it at him yelling for him to stop. He did. He started to cry.

*

Yveline Walker called the only cop she trusted. Tony had not yet started his night shift but he quickly came to her Ferndale Street home anyway.

"I got your phone message Yveline."

"Come in Tony please."

"You said your nephew was arrested?"

"By the FBI. Now they say he is being released and I should pick him up. Will you go with me?"

"Of course. Did they tell you why he was arrested?"

"They said he was a suspect in a terrorist plot."

"But they are releasing him?"

"What choice do they have? This is absurd."

"Tell me what you know."

"I sent him on an errand. Part of the reason he is staying with me is because he is agropho…?

"Agoraphobic? Afraid of the outside."

"Yes. His mother believes I can help him. We have him on a new medication for his epilepsy. He has had frequent violent seizures all his life. That is why he became afraid to venture from the house. The new medication is miraculous. He still has seizures but they are mild. Rarely does he experience anything more than a momentary trance. He doesn't fall down or shake violently."

"What was the errand?"

"I sent him to pick up a package for me. It would have been the longest walk he ever had taken by himself."

"What was in the package?"

"He was supposed to pick up my pressed and folded blouses at the cleaners."

"Let's go get him," Tony said without disguising the dismay on his face. "And your laundry."

*

Thomas and Leon each stuffed a handgun into their trouser waistline and headed out of the Allston apartment together. Two problems left. Two guns. Two solutions. Easy. Just in case, Thomas sent Leon back inside to get the AK-47. They got into the Altima and drove in silence to Codman Square.

CHAPTER 48

It had been a long but satisfying Friday. They'd spent the entire day together using a City Hall conference room as a dual command center. The tentacles of the child slave-trade bust in Dorchester reached into other realms and neighborhoods. Invaluable information provided by the Mali woman and her son Ali, from protective custody after their hospital stay, led to fifteen arrests. With the leads Sanchez provided, arrests were underway in five cities coast to coast.

Sean really liked Suzanne Sanchez. It helped that there was a certain solidarity in their work. She cared. Homeland was organized to truly think globally and act locally. The FBI was arrogant, self-aggrandizing and Washington-centric, like the Bersconis who put a face on it. Worse maybe were the Stearns of the State Department who were duplicitous by nature. More concerned with duping scientists to help some South American nation with forest stabilization than helping people. Their do-good ecologists never realized they were just mules transporting top-secret documents for covert operations.

"Can I buy you a drink?" Sean said, remembering too late that he had promised to call Ketia for one today.

Suzanne hesitated before replying. She didn't see this coming.

"I know a swell little café in the North End with sidewalk tables. Great place to sip wine and watch the people flow by."

"Yes. I'd like that. I'd like that very much."

"Shall we walk?" said Sean holding open the door. He thought of Ketia and how she was playing him against Tony's son. Two can play that game he told himself.

*

Leon got out on New England Avenue near the corner of Southern at five minutes before eight. Thomas drove away and would return to pick him up in fifteen minutes. He felt conspicuous with his bushy red beard and bald head even though the street was dark. In his jacket he carried a Russian-made semi-automatic pistol with a silencer. He'd only seen Dougherty once from a distance but that was sufficient. He walked around the corner and headed down Southern Avenue. An unchained Doberman stretched out on a porch raised its head.

"Easy fella," Leon said. The dog relaxed and put its head back down. "See you in ten minutes," Leon said.

*

Dougherty was told to meet Thomas at 8 pm in a vacant first floor flat on Southern Avenue. Andrea Coles had an officer drive Dougherty's car from the Herald to the address. The officer in the car looked just like Dougherty with the wig, cap and appropriate clothes over his body armor. Dougherty left the Herald unnoticed from a side entrance and got into Cole's unmarked vehicle.

Andrea and Tony set up a command in the vacant second floor flat of a derelict property across the street from the address. At 8 pm a red-bearded bald man came walking down the street and entered the flat where the decoy was positioned.

Detective Coles signaled Dougherty to come to the window. "Is that Thomas?" she said.

"No. Never saw this guy before," Dougherty said.

Coles radioed the Dougherty imposter in the flat about the development. After a long pause he answered back that the he and the SWAT team had just arrested the bearded fellow without incident for carrying a concealed weapon.

"No one's read him his rights yet," Coles said as she turned her attention away from the radio and to Tony who had been busy on another frequency. "But he's not talking anyway, and he has no identification."

Tony was about to reply when more radio traffic filled the space.

"C11. Unit six. Picked him up at Gallivan. Still refusing to yield."

"C11. Unit ten. Setting up road block Washington at Rugsdale Road."

"I gotta go on this one," he said. "See if you can get red beard to talk."

*

Thomas parked by the plumbing supply shop on Washington Street at eight sharp. Meacham was standing in front waiting. Thomas had stopped by earlier to be sure the door was unlocked and the vacant shop unoccupied.

"Where's the supply?" Meacham said, noting Thomas was empty handed.

"Inside," Thomas said, holding open the door for Meacham and then closing it behind them.

Five seconds later Thomas emerged and got into his car. As he drove away a patrol car pulled in behind him and activated the light bar. Thomas floored the accelerator pedal.

The light at the intersection of Gallivan Boulevard was red but Thomas blew through it. He saw cop cars blocking the road ahead and was trying to make a u-turn when he blew a tire. His car skidded sideways and crashed into a pole. The cops were all around him within moments. Thomas grabbed the AK-47 from the passenger side floor and dove out into the street. He rolled and came up firing. For an instant he thought he was going to get away. The next instant he was dead.

*

By the time Tony arrived at the scene there were plenty of officers. The situation was already stabilizing under the direction of another Sergeant.

"Ambulance is here Sarge, but it ain't doin this one no good," the young officer said as he was going through the contents of the Altima.

"I picked him up on routine patrol. I've been keeping an eye on that plumbing shop like you asked, Sarge. I just wanted to ask him what he was doing there. He took off and then came out shooting. We had to take him down," the young officer explained.

"Who do we have?" Tony said.

"His driver license says he is Thomas Reid but it's a forgery. There's a briefcase in the trunk with two passports. One could be him. We're running it."

Tony nodded without replying as he was engaged with a cell phone call from an officer at the plumbing shop.

"Confirming we have a fresh body here with a gunshot wound to the head. Identification says he is one Michael Hannan Meacham," he heard the officer say. "And yeah he's the doctor from the Talbot Institute and MGH."

"Middle name Hannan? Ending with A N?" Tony said.

"That's right."

"Strange," Tony said.

"Hey kid," Tony called over to the officer with the passports. "You know back before this was called Washington Street. It was called the Upper Road. A business man named Hannan lived right about on this spot. What do you think about that?"

The young officer didn't. Sergeant Sebastiene always had a history lesson. They learned to ignore him.

Tony looked at the piece of paper Yveline Walker had given him, then at the plate of the Nissan Altima.

"XLB 713," he said, filling in Yveline's blank space with numbers 1 and 3.

"Hey kid, who's the vehicle registered to?" Tony said.

"A Leon Howe with an Allston address. Here's his passport."

Tony looked at the picture of the red-bearded bald man and punched speed dial on his cell.

"Coles," she answered. "What's up Tony?

"Tell Leon Red Beard his friend Thomas is dead and I'm heading to his place in Allston soon as I pick up the warrant," Tony said. "See what he has to say about that. And tell that reporter Dougherty he better get moving. His story is running away from him."

CHAPTER 49

Quietly he closed the door to his North End apartment. He locked the chain as if it could help make this Saturday morning a long and leisurely one. He placed the cappuccinos and the morning paper on the small kitchen table. Stripping off his jogging suit he took a quick shower. Returning to the kitchen in his robe he saw Suzanne standing at the bedroom threshold wearing one of his flannel shirts. Despite his efforts at being quiet he'd awakened her.

"Here," he said handing her one of the cappuccinos he'd bought at the corner café. "You almost look awake. This will help."

"Good morning," she said. "Thanks." She turned and walked to the bedroom window sipping her coffee. "Looks like a nice day."

Sean entered the bedroom and tossed the Globe onto the end of the bed.

HUMAN TRAFFICKING OPERATION RAIDED IN DORCHESTER

"Look at the story below the fold," he said.

LOCAL FBI MISTAKE STRANGLES COMMUTE
Red Line Shut Down For Hours

"Bersconi made a fool of himself profiling black kids in hoodies. But now for the hat trick," said Sean.

He threw the Herald down next to the Globe.

EXCLUSIVE
BOSTON POLICE FOIL TERRORIST PLOT
By Matthew Dougherty

Suzanne put down the coffee and picked up the Herald and read aloud. "Containers of deadly avian flu virus recovered from Allston residence. Chemist arrest at Logan Airport leads to extremist cell in Brooklyn. Plan to disperse virus at Grand Central Station averted. FBI arrests ringleaders."

"That would be the New York Special Agent-in-Charge making the arrest. Courtesy of the Boston Police Department. They went at it all night." Sean said.

"Like we didn't," she said dropping the paper to the floor along with the flannel shirt.

Sean slipped off his robe and stepped toward her. She dodged left, dropping her weight as her hands grabbed his right forearm and wrist. He was six years her junior, and more current with the academy training, but she remembered how to execute a take down move.

As he fell backward onto the bed he kicked out and rolled, using her force as momentum in a counter move. He spun her onto her back and then straddled her on the bed.

Right where she wanted him.

"What's a hat trick?" she said.

CHAPTER 50

"Ketia Depestre approached me after class with a unique personal problem," Melissa White said to her husband from her sofa seat.

"Lovely, bright young lady. I really enjoyed talking with her at the Dean's social last month. Of course her problems would be unique. Here. We're trying Pappy Van Winkle Kentucky bourbon for a change of pace. Had to be wait-listed at the shop to get a bottle," Edmund said as he placed two tumblers on the coffee table.

"You may know she volunteers at a Health Center in Dorchester. An associate there came across a family document. A trust document of sorts. Bearer to inherit a stake in the defunct Baker's Chocolate factory."

"Lower Mills? That closed in 1965 or so."

"Right. And the document is early 1800."

"It can't possibly still be valid."

"That's what I said. But Ketia connected some dots. By the time the factory closed, the company was owned by General Foods. A benefactor of the Health Center is a client of yours and..."

"Gordon Chamberlain. Of course. Kraft bought General Foods before he retired. While he was still on their Board. I remember that from his portfolio. Still, I don't see how…with all the changes in laws and corporations…it would be possible to determine a value, even if it is valid. But it is worth taking a look at. Get it for me and I'll show it to Gordon."

"We hoped you'd say that," Melissa said as she carefully handed him the document sheathed in protective plastic.

*

Ms. Sheila Waters, descendant of Baina/Sarah and her daughter Katherine Preston, was not only an avid volunteer and Board member at the Health Center, she was also a distant cousin to Ketia. At Tony's request Ketia was able to arrange a meeting at Ms. Waters Codman Hill home. Both Tony and

Finn balked at the involvement of a Vodoun priest, but Ms. Waters insisted. The priest was affiliated with her Haitian church. He also held degrees in both anthropology and archaeology.

The museum crate had been delivered several days earlier. Ms. Waters had familiarized herself with its contents.

"The authenticity of the Baker Company document is being researched," she said. "I am told it is authentic, and its value holds promise."

She lifted and displayed the photo that had contained the document.

"This is a photo of my great aunt. She never married and lived alone on Talbot Avenue. She was trained as a Vodoun priestess but to my knowledge never practiced. I remember going over to her house once or twice as a child. She was distant but nice. The chest contains her possessions. She suffered dementia in her later years and became unable to care for herself. A cousin had her committed to an institution. I am saddened to say that the family abandoned her."

"Did you find any of the other items to be of value?" Tony said.

"Well there is some sentimental value. No artifacts other than the box." She looked to the priest.

"If I may intercede," the tall young man in loose fitting white cotton garb took his cue. "I am not important. Neither is this box. But your relationship with it, especially you Ms. Waters, is powerful. The inscriptions are Veve, a beacon for the loa, the spirit.

In this case a loa carried with the Atlantic slave trade."

The priest solicited individual eye contact of all in the room.

"May I open this?"

No one dissuaded him. He studied the box for a minute, turning it this way and that not unlike a Rubik's cube. Suddenly it was open revealing two irregular halves, the deeper of which contained a bone fragment and a piece of crystal.

"The museum scanner showed the box to be empty," said Tony, barely concealing his surprise.

"Machine screwed up," said Finn.

"Machines see what those who make them want them to see," said the priest. "These items travelled a long way to this final destination. They did not travel as objects but as manifestation of spirit."

The priest looked at Sheila Waters, commanding her attention.

"This box represents many dreams. These can be hopeful dreams come true, or great nightmares."

"What would you have me do?" Sheila Waters said.

"Are you content with your life?" the priest said.

"Reasonably, yes."

"Then we shall burn it" he replied.

He led them all to the back porch where he had prepared a fire in a small chiminea.

The priest handed the pieces of bone and crystal to Ms. Waters. Wordlessly he closed the box and placed it in the fire. They all watched for a few minutes as it flamed and disintegrated. He walked away.

"This guy comes prepared," Tony whispered to Finn.

"Depends on the situation," Finn whispered back. "Wouldn't invite him to a cookout with the Eire Pub crowd."

CHAPTER 51

Ketia and Melissa White both glanced at the monitor displaying Ann's wavering vitals, then quickly back to the patient whose left arm moved slightly. Ketia reached out and gently grasped her hand and wrist in search of a pulse.

"You took my hand," they both heard Ann whisper.

Then she was gone.

The long-term care facility where she had resided before coming to Talbot had recently turned over some additional records that were long lost. A generous South Shore man, named Robert Winston, had married Ann's mother, Irene Connolly, while Ann was still in her teens. Winston felt strongly that Ann's care would be better covered under his policies if he adopted her. At that time they changed her name to Winston. The records listed Winston and his wife as deceased along with the only other next-of-kin, brother Jack and father Frank.

Ketia left to call the undertaker. With Meacham dead she'd also need to bring in an on-call physician to sign the death certificate. Since there were no relatives to contact, a simple cremation would be paid for by the Institute.

Melissa White looked at Ann's charts. The familiar recurring patterns looped through her final dreaming hours. In her final minutes the pattern changed. The graph climbed and erratically peaked and fell, repeatedly and rapidly.

"Her dream changed," she said to Ketia who was no longer there.

The Harvard class was attentive as Professor White recapped the entire course in her closing remarks. This was her final lecture of the semester in the popular *Quantum Perspective in Dream Psychology* elective. Even Harold was silent.

"We reviewed the historical importance of dreams throughout all cultures. Language, as it reflects human thought, continues to affirm this importance. And yet, science relegates the dream realm to the study of brain stem nerve agitations.

We have looked at how consciousness shapes the brain. We acknowledge that we can direct our dreams. In dreams we visit bizarre landscapes and engage all manner of people, some dead and some unknown. There is no physical basis for this realm to exist. It is all in the mind.

This so infuriates our science that the best answer we can provide is that consciousness has no purpose in the known universe. But we are not conscious in dreams. Not conscious in this place outside the known universe of science. We go there anyway.

We reviewed waking dream states. Trances and such. We found the portal experience of the light at the end of the tunnel to be most powerful in the cultural lore. Our science cannot even explain where light originates. Let alone how light finds a way into our dreams.

We reviewed quantum states and found that every particle, EVERYTHING, has the capacity to be in two places at the same time. Science reluctantly concurs.

And today we looked at time itself. How it evolved in just recent centuries as an important but purely human construct. So important to the way we think that the relative nature of space and time emerging from Einstein's work confounds us with its paradox. Our science would have us cower in denial rather than confront our human condition.

Time is flexible, but it is inseparable from space. Time has a different relevance for every two connecting points. It has a different relevance for every string connecting the observer and the observed.

In space-time next year already exists. Last year is still around. There is no NOW in space-time.

How can science tell us there is no NOW, yet not explain why we experience otherwise?

How? Because contemporary science only addresses the physical realm. Consider once more that dreams have no physical basis. In dreams a NOW can and does exist. Why? Because there is no space-time in dreams. Dreams do not occur in a physical realm.

I leave you with a reflection for your lives beyond this classroom. It will not appear on the final exam. But I ask you to ponder this… As our science of space and time overlooks our realm of dreams, just how might our dream realm enrich our science of time and space?

Questions?"

*

He couldn't move or speak. He could hear urgent voices. He was being pushed, prodded. All he could see was blinding white light. Then she took his hand. Or did he take hers?

Snapping out of his happy daydream he turned on his pocket transistor radio just as Red Sox fireman Dick Radatz climbed upon the mound to try to close a rare win over the perennial champion Yankees. Mike was still smiling about the kiss Annie sneaked onto his cheek as they said their goodbyes at her doorstep. Walking home he noticed Annie's little brother Jack Connolly about a block up Southern Avenue coming toward him. Between he and Jack was a tall skinny kid with a smaller companion. Mike felt a sense of ominous menace as they approached Jack. He was about to shout out when they abruptly crossed the street, turned a corner and disappeared. The ill feeling dissipated.

"Hey Jack!," Mike called out as they passed each other on opposite sides of the street.

"Ya?" replied Jack, somewhat shy of the older guy.

"My parents are taking me and your sister to the beach at Brant Rock tomorrow morning. Wanna come with us?"

"For sure. That'd be pissa!"

"Okay, so you and Annie be at my house by nine. Oh, and you gotta do me a favor."

"What?"

"Tell your sister I said she's the prettiest girl in Codman Square."

Jack moved on and Mike looked up at the summer sky. It seemed particularly bright. He closed his eyes and basked in the warmth.

"He's gone," Ketia said. She let go of Mike's hand and pulled the sheet over his head.

*

"How did the final lecture go today Professor Leary?" Edmund White joked as he joined Melissa in their parlor.

"Probably not well enough to carry the class into next year's curriculum."

"But the students love it!"

"True as that is, I just can't produce supporting research in time to save it. Although an interesting development this afternoon at the Institute looks promising."

"Let's hear," said Edmund placing his glass onto the coffee table.

"We'll first of all I'm sorry to say we lost two patients today. Ann Winston and Gordon's ward, Michael Scanlon."

"Gordon will be upset. Did you…"

"Yes. I called him immediately. Everything is fine on that count."

"Then what is so promising?"

"Well I'd taken to charting Scanlon's dreams. Remarkably he had the same recurring pattern as Ann Winston. I discussed this with Michael a few days before he was killed. He said it was not the coma causing the repetitive dreams but more likely the mechanism of injury, or events just preceding it. Same as he said about Ann Winston."

"Do you know the mechanism of injury?"

"He was shot in the head."

"He would have been just a boy. You mean he lay there in a coma having the same dream over and over all those years?"

"Apparently, we can't be sure, but here's the promising part. I just found out that Ann Winston, Annie Connolly in 1965, was in the next room in a Quincy apartment when Scanlon was shot back then. Today, when she died, he was in the next room at Talbot. He died less than two minutes after her."

"What caused his death?"

"Natural causes, but of course the physician had to ascribe renal failure or something specific, but I'd say he just followed his dream."

"Followed his dream?"

"Yes, in his final minutes his dream changed. Same pattern as with Ann Winston. There has to be something publishable there. A thread. I just need more time."

"Why so? You have the transcripts from Sam Stockton to support your theory."

"Afraid not. Our tech guy discovered Meacham had altered those. Fabricated is perhaps the better word."

"But why?"

"We'll never know but I suspect to set me up as a fraud if I published. My funding would dry up and Meacham could then have easily forced me out of the Institute and have it all to himself. Like I said…I need more time."

"And that, sweetheart, is something you of all people, should have in infinite supply."

CHAPTER 52

The burial service for Annie and Mike completed, Finn and Tony made their way toward Codman's tomb and the cemetery exit gate.

"Why didn't you tell me Mike was still alive?" Finn said.

"I thought you knew. Guess while you were away at that auto mechanic school for juvenile delinquents you missed the memo."

"Being?"

"That this rich guy named Gordon Chamberlain took over Mike Scanlon's care back then. Same guy who just insisted Mike be laid to rest here in his childhood neighborhood."

"You know this guy?"

"I've seen him. Said hello. He's also the same guy who moved the Baker deed along for Sheila Waters."

"So when he heard the story about Annie he halted the cremation and had her laid to rest in this adjoining plot?"

"You got it. A regular guardian angel." Tony nodded his head toward Codman's burial mound. "I wasn't sure you'd come here," he said.

Finn continued to look straight ahead. "Nightmares are gone," he said.

"Can I speak with you guys a minute?" Dougherty said from behind them.

They paused with the Herald reporter in front of Codman's tomb.

"You know your friend broke the Guinness record by almost four years?" Dougherty said.

"That so," Finn said.

"Woman named Elaine Esposito lasted forty-three years in a coma. Remember back in the 1990's the Terri Schiavo case in Florida?"

No one answered but Dougherty continued undaunted. "Big controversy about sustaining her in a persistent vegetative state. Anyway they both died while being cared for in Pinellas County, Florida. They both had the same birthday. Know what else?"

Again no answer. "Doctor Michael Meacham was working in Pinellas at the time. Maybe doing some experiments? Spooky huh?"

"What do you want Dougherty? Your big scoop not good enough for you? You gonna do a tabloid sensational for an encore?" Tony said.

"Alright. Here's where I'm really going. Juvenile records are sealed but the press was a little more lenient back in the day," Dougherty said.

"Yeah?" Tony said with an edge.

"So I looked at the microfiche of the old Boston Record American newspaper. Seems some teenagers named Antoine Sebastiene and Finn Leahy were involved in a certain Quincy shooting back in 1965."

"So what more do you need Dougherty? You got the whole story. It just ended," Tony said turning away.

"Oh I got the beginning and the end alright. I think there's a whole lot more in the middle what makes the story happen."

"Damned if that ain't always the way. Good luck Mr. Dougherty," Finn said as he and Tony walked away.

CHAPTER 53

Gordon Chamberlain had not hesitated to present the 1803 deed to his friends at Kraft. Corporate counsel found it both perplexing and archaic, but recommended settlement nonetheless. The Board voted to purchase the document as a company museum piece from Sheila Waters for five-hundred-thousand dollars, and to donate one million dollars to the Health Center. Gordon matched that amount.

After the November elections the President and a slightly-less dysfunctional Congress were somehow able to pass a jobs bill. The Act created jobs in distressed neighborhoods, specifically addressing health care and education. The grant process was streamlined. Massachusetts was among the states clearly favored. Already the economic climate of Codman Square had turned a corner. The President even cited the neighborhood in a nationally televised speech as an example of success.

Tony was able to retire from the police force. Almost. Sean arranged the creation of a special task force to keep Codman Square crime free. Detective Andrea Coles was promoted and appointed to head it up. Sean convinced Tony to sign on part-time as a retired annuitant to help make the effort successful.

Nothing had ever bothered Tony quite as much as finding slave trading in his own neighborhood. He thought America had long ago turned the page on that ugly chapter. He was proud that Africans built this country. First as slaves then as laborers. Now, even as a President. Damned if they were going to come back to America again as slaves. Not in Codman Square. Not on his watch.

Tony talked Finn into accepting seed money from Gordon Chamberlain to obtain matching funds from a federal opportunity grant and start an automotive mechanics school in the abandoned restaurant-supply warehouse on New England Avenue. A non-profit was established in partnership with Boston Public Schools. Students got a stipend to attend and received academic credit. Math and science class curriculums were aligned with the effort. Students had to maintain a passing GPA to stay in the class. Organizations donated clunkers for them to repair. Graduating seniors received their own set of wheels that they had personally restored. Jobs were offered through partnership programs in the greater metropolitan area.

Females were welcome, and a few did attend, but a parallel program was established by Sheila Waters through the Health Center Foundation, also in partnership with Boston Public Schools. Apprenticeships at Carney Hospital lead to health care jobs. Some guys opted for this route also.

If eradicating the evil of slavery, and breaking the resultant cycle of poverty in Codman Square, required the effort of building a castle then Tony figured he had already placed the first brick.

Crime was down dramatically in the neighborhood. Social organizations were thriving. Everyone who needed health care got it. There was a jobs corp for teens. Small businesses thrived. It was as if a curse had been lifted.

CHAPTER 54

His shift over, Tony walked down the hill on his way home from the Health Center. As he crossed Southern Avenue and came to the odd shaped church that was once Kaspar Brothers Market a wave of nostalgia washed over him. He thought again of all the games and mischief that happened around this little island of bricks and mortar. Where did it all go, he wondered. Where did all the time go?

As if on cue his grandson Petey ran around a corner of Kaspar's island and quickly out of sight in some game of chase with a white boy about his age, which was ten.

"White kid," Tony said almost aloud. "Rare sight this side of the Square." Then he froze. It was as if time had stopped. The kid looked exactly as he remembered Mike Scanlon so long ago.

"Irish kids all look alike," he said to himself unconvincingly.

Petey came running by again. This time his cousin Felix giving chase.

"Hey Grampa," Petey shouted out as he sped away.

"Hey to you too. What happened to your other friend, little guy?" Tony called after him.

The two boys stopped and looked back at him quizzically. Then they were off again. Tony stared after them.

"Whoa," said his neighbor Howard, a burly middle-aged black man with paint splattered overalls, also making his way home from work. "Someone put a hex on you."

Tony's eyes came back into focus and he realized he had been standing there with his mind somewhere else. He smiled and nodded as Howard moved on.

"Hey Howard!" Tony called out. "You smell that?"

"Smell what?" Howard said.

He looked back momentarily at Tony. Lips pursed. Brow furrowed. Shaking his head side to side he moved on again.

Tony stood there a while longer as the light coastal breeze passed.

A faint scent of roasting chocolate lingered in the air.

About the author

J.R. Quirk lives in Fallbrook, California with Priscilla Lyons, his college sweetheart.

A graduate of Harvard College, he holds a Masters degree in psychology from George Mason University.

Before retiring to write fiction and create music, he worked as a park ranger and superintendent in the forests, deserts, mountains, beaches, wetlands, and historic parks of California, and as a National Park Superintendent for historic New Orleans.

Made in the USA
Middletown, DE
06 August 2015